CHARLIE GLASS

REVISITED

PART TWO OF THE
CHARLIE GLASS SERIES

AN ORIGINAL NOVEL BY
BUD SELIGSON

The following original novel has been copyrighted and registered with the Writer's Guild of America-West under the name of Bud Seligson

Cover Art and Interior design by: Cyrusfiction Productions.

First Edition
ISBN: 978-1-946480-20-0

9018 Balboa Boulevard
Suite #562
Northridge, CA 91325

DEDICATION PAGE

With the exception of doing the research and touring locations, the life of a writer tends to be very solitary and often quite boring!

Never more so for me as when I am working under a deadline!

Every year, my wife Diane puts up with the long hours, and the fact that even when I am home, I am often mentally elsewhere!

I am a lucky man to be married to such an awesome, and understanding woman.

—Bud Seligson

INTRODUCTION

A SHORT NOTE OF APPRECIATION FROM AUTHOR BUD

This is indeed a work of pure fiction, and perhaps more so than is usual for me. Almost nothing in the following hundreds of pages will be based upon any sort of reality whatsoever. Accuracy was not deemed crucial, and long paragraphs of make-believe were used to avoid looking up facts.

Inevitably through, even the most professional of writers, must always have a foundation for their creations, and I was occasionally at a loss as to where and when to place my characters.

And so I did what any intelligent writer should do. I turned to my editor-in-chief and dear friend James Crewe, who without a moment's hesitation came to my aid and suggested a twist here and a turn there, and everything suddenly turned out to be just right!

And so, to you, my dear fellow, I offer up my everlasting friendship and awe at the knowledge that resides at your fingertips, which you are always ready to share.

§

Not that it really matters, but this is the second of four planned Charlie Glass stories.

When. I mustered up the discipline to write a Los Angeles Sheriff's Department type of murder/suspense adventure, I cast around for a hero who was cut from a different mold. I wanted to create someone with rough edges, yet who would have a great degree of style. My hero had to feel equally at ease entertaining a gorgeous woman at a fine restaurant, or just downing a beer with the boys. He had to be a congenial kind of guy, with a tinge of mystery about him.

Instead of a gambling casino, like a James Bond, or the streets of New York, like many of our fiction heroes, his territory became the classic Los Angeles Sheriff's Department, and his challenge was solving the unknown.

The Lone Ranger had Tonto, and the Green Hornet had Kato, but does our Charlie really have the ever-faithful Joe Wahl or Roberto Sanchez at his side?

Let us find out.

Thanks, and I wish you a good read!

—Bud Seligson

THE FOLLOWING EXCERPT IS FROM THE LAST
CHAPTER OF BOOK ONE OF THE CHARLIE GLASS
SERIES, *CHARLIE GLASS: A SHATTERING EXPERIENCE*"

A command post was set up by the ticket-booth area where the pier started out toward the ocean. An overwhelming show of force was accumulated there, with the Sheriff's Department, the LAPD, the SWAT team and members of the local Santa Monica Police all present and eager to get involved. The Fire Department was soon to arrive also.

A note was handed to Charlie from one of his field officers, who had a message for him from Central Control. It was from Sweetpea, who had received an incoming call at her office from Leonardo da Vinci. It asked if Charlie would please call him on his unlisted cellphone so that they could talk things over before everything got unpleasant.

Charlie immediately called the number and heard da Vinci's loud, deep voice answering.

It was agreed that they would meet in the center of the pier at the merry-go-round, which da Vinci told him was always his favorite ride because it went around and around. They also agreed that they would each bring a second person with them, and da Vinci asked if Charlie would kindly bring him a large cup of coffee with two creams.

Charlie, who was loving the balls that this guy was showing, agreed to bring the coffee and said that it would take him a little bit of time getting it.

da Vinci, laughing, told him that there was no hurry, and that he had no other place to go. He would see Charlie and one other as they walked toward the merry-go-round meeting place.

They both agreed not to bring weapons with them.

As Charlie sent one of the policemen to get a cup of coffee with two creams, he went into the Sheriff's command trailer with Joe Wahl and Roberto Sanchez to talk things over. Charlie wanted to watch each man closely as they talked He was hoping one of the two would give himself away.

Once they were seated and all other persons were sent out of the trailer, they first agreed that Roberto's SWAT team leader, Ron Sellz, would accompany Charlie to the meeting. Ron Sellz was highly trained and could sense a set-up that could go wrong instantly. Charlie accepted the suggestion.

The three of them agreed that Charlie should offer da Vinci a peaceful surrender, hopefully with no one on either side getting hurt. They all said that they would go along with giving Da Vince a better surrender deal if he would talk about the organized crime set-up in the city.

It was Roberto Sanchez who surprised Charlie when he suggested that he place one of his best sharpshooters to keep da Vinci in sight just in case he was going to try something.

Charlie thought that Joe would have asked for the sharpshooter so that he could have da Vinci killed at his command when he could say that he saw da Vinci make a threatening move toward Charlie. Charlie was confused as he still did not know just who the mole was—and none of this was helpful.

The coffee with two creams arrived along with officer Ron Sellz, and the three men shook hands, and Ron Sellz and Charlie Glass once again put their lives on the line as they walked toward the merry-go-round in the distance. The normal night lights were on all over the pier area, and walking toward the merry-go-round was not a problem.

With coffee in hand Charlie and Ron Sellz stood there as Leonardo da Vinci and another nameless man stepped out of the shadows and into the light where they all looked at each other.

Charlie made the first move, which was to hand over the cup of coffee that he was holding, and he received a polite thank-you.

Charlie took his time as he looked over at Leonardo da Vinci XVIII and found him to still be a tall, dark and very handsome man, who seemed comfortable just standing there sipping at his coffee. It was very interesting to Charlie how da Vinci could look so elegant and relaxed when he must realize that he was a hunted man, and that his world of created fear, crime and hustling for a living was crumbling all around him.

It was da Vinci's suggestion that he and Charlie walk over to the standing merry-go-round and sit and talk things over. Each of them asked their seconds to stand by, and quite pleasantly, side by side, they calmly walked over to the merry-go-round, where they each selected a horse to sit sidesaddle on.

Charlie just knew in his gut that da Vinci would choose a horse that was higher up in its frozen position, and would indicate one which was somewhat lower for Charlie to sit on. Charlie smiled to himself. This guy was still role-playing and always seemed to like being the "higher up."

Charlie did not care either way and just took his saddle seat and waited for da Vinci to open up the conversation. As da Vinci had said earlier, there was no hurry.

"Charlie Glass is an interesting name for a policeman," da Vinci began. "It is a name that one can see through." He smiled his great smile at his own humor. "I have heard from my sources that you have been searching for me and the mole that you think is in your ranks, and I believe that I can help you with that, since your mole is my mole, so to speak.

"I find it most interesting how you have turned loose your new 'Gangster Squad' against me and made the good citizens of Los Angeles eager to turn in my collectors.

"I absolutely do agree with you that it is time for organized crime to remove ourselves out of your city for a while. We can always come back at a later date when the people won't be so happy with the police as they are now.

"So here is my proposal. You arrest me and my men and make a big showing out of it. Who knows; maybe I can be of help getting you elected as Sheriff of your fair city.

"You charge us and escort us to the state line and make a big deal of it all, and in return I will, on that last day that we will ever see each other, whisper in your ear the name of the person who was working with your Captain Crewe for many years while he was helping my organization at the same time. And by the way, I really liked your gun to the ear campaign that you did a while back. It really got everybody talking about you.

"So, I give you your mole with proof of who he is, and you let my men and me go. Does this sound like a workable compromise to you? Putting me in jail does nothing to help you, and getting out of town will give me a new place to travel. We have a win-win situation if you will agree."

Charlie looked at da Vinci for a few moments, stood up and walked back to where his back-up man, Ron Sellz, and the second guy with da Vinci was standing.

Charlie knew that he was going to take the deal. There was really no downside for himself, and getting rid of the mole that was driving him crazy would be wonderful. He would be happy to let da Vinci get out of town and bother someone else. This would be some sort of a twisted justice thing after all.

He walked over to where da Vinci and his backup guy were standing, and put out his hand for da Vinci to shake, when a shot rang out and da Vinci crumpled to the ground with a perfectly round hole in the very center of his forehead. It was located just where a sharpshooter would center his shot.

As da Vinci collapsed, the blood from the wound splattered all over and covered Charlie from head to foot.

Charlie was in shock. Did the sharpshooter think that when da Vinci was putting out his hand to shake Charlie's hand on the agreement, that he had a knife or was attacking Charlie, and to defend the detective he had launched the shot in defense of him?

Charlie would never know, as he just stood there and looked down at the now lifeless body of Leonardo da Vinci XVIII bleeding out in front of him and the merry-go-round.

§

Three days had passed quickly and Charlie finally had a bit of peace and quiet as he sat at his desk and kept going over the events of the past few days.

He was being called a hero for removing the threat that da Vinci and his criminal Organization cast over the Los Angeles area. The Mayor and the remaining City Council members had authorized a special award event to present Charlie with a medal of honor for having cleaned up the city.

This was wonderful, and Charlie appreciated all the things happening around him, but, as he told Sweetpea, da Vinci's death stopped the discovery of who the mole was.

When Charlie had talked with the sharpshooter who had fired that deadly bullet, the soldier had told him that his orders were to keep his rifle aimed at da Vinci at all times. He was well trained and never would have taken that one deadly shot if he was not ordered to do so.

Who gave that order will never be known because both Joe Wahl and Roberto Sanchez were both standing behind him watching Charlie as he was talking with da Vinci. With all the noise and activity going on around them, the concentrating shooter heard a command that came from right behind him. "SHOOT! SHOOT NOW."

Within moments of the deadly shot being fired, everyone rushed forward to aid Charlie if he needed it, and the shooter could not tell who it was that said those deadly words.

When the board of inquiry briefly looked into the matter, both Joe Wahl and Roberto Sanchez denied giving the order, and with the confusion that was going on at that moment in time, no one other that the shooter heard those words spoken, and the matter was closed, with great relief on everyone's part. da Vinci and the Mob were now gone from the city and everyone was pleased.

Everyone except Charlie, because the solution to his problem with the mole was still ongoing.

Both Joe and Roberto seemed pleased that everything was coming to an end and that Charlie remained unhurt. But for Charlie, nothing really was resolved. The mole lived on and he had yet to figure out who it was.

With the two lead detectives still working with him, Charlie felt that he was personally involved in a classic the-lady-or-the-tiger scenario that had taken up his interest in a college course he took in his rookie year as a Sheriff's deputy. The lady or the tiger? is a classical situation that definitely applied to Charlie and his frustrating problem.

"The Lady or the Tiger?" is a famous short story that was first published in 1882, and Charlie remembered every single word of it. The story had entered the English language as a person's problem with a situation that is not solvable.

The short story takes place in a land ruled by a semi-barbaric king who had some very progressive ideas, and some other thoughts that would cause people to suffer. The most famous of the king's ideas was to create a public arena to use a trial by ordeal as his justice system. The person's crime would be judged for punishment or innocence as decided by the rule of chance.

When the protagonist of the story was accused of a crime, his future was to be judged in the public arena where he would be made to stand before two closed doors.

Behind one door was a young lady who the king had deemed a good match for the accused. Behind the other was a fierce and very hungry tiger!

The accused was compelled to select one of the two doors. If he chose the door with the lady behind it, he would be found innocent and must immediately marry the lady. But if he choose the door with the tiger behind it, he of course was deemed guilty and was immediately devoured by the tiger.

Charlie knew that it was a simple story with an ending that would bring a particular problem to an end, one way or the other. The person was either innocent or guilty. End of discussion.

Charlie also had two doors behind which his two suspects were standing. One of them was innocent and one of them was not. It was Charlie that had to make the decision, and he hated having to do it without more information, and so he decided to do nothing about the mole until something came up that would give him away.

Until that time, Charlie went back to work.

CHARLIE GLASS
REVISITED

AN ORIGINAL NOVEL BY
BUD SELIGSON

CHAPTER ONE

Al Capone (1899–1947) had a favorite expression that still works today: "You can get a lot farther with a kind word and a gun than with a kind word alone."

§

A smiling Charlie Glass opened up his lecture series being held in the basement assembly room of the Los Angeles County Sheriff's Department's Central Downtown Jail. A very attentive audience was perfectly silent as Charlie went into his prepared presentation entitled "Getting Connected, and How It All Began."

"The thing about mobsters in the late 1950s was that you could count on them to be absolutely consistent. They were very predictable. In those days, five crime families ruled over the city of New York: Gambino, Lucchese, Colombo, Bonanno and Genovese—and they in turn were overseen by a commission. Nothing ever happened without the others being kept informed about what each of them were doing.

"When the Bonannos shipped heroin into Montreal to smuggle into the states, the other four families stayed completely away from Montreal. When the Gambinos ran a tax-fraud racket on Long Island, the others again stayed away. When one of the families negotiated an alliance with hoods in Buffalo or Detroit or New

Orleans, the other four stayed away from Buffalo, Detroit, or New Orleans. It was a gentlemen's business completely orchestrated by men who were anything but gentle. Every now and then, however, there would be a falling-out, and two or more of the families would 'go to the mattresses.' One bunch of idiots would start shooting at another bunch of idiots.

"Civilians and family members, namely wives and children, were unconditionally off limits at all times, and as bodies littered the streets, the New York Police Department would take an unofficial step back. They would let the bad guys kill one another until the crime commission to whom they answered enforced a truce among them. The New York Police Department would then count the bodies, and someone in the department would inevitably declare to the press, 'As far as we are concerned that is twenty-two fewer gangsters for us to worry about'—and then they would pack the bodies off to the local morgue. The 'badfellows' would return to being 'goodfellows,' and everyone would wait patiently for the next time. There was a complete order to all of this, a coherence that somehow made a lot of sense to one and all. This 'goodfellows/badfellows' all became part of the myth, the stuff that the *Godfather* movies were made from.

"And then there came upon the scene one very special man who changed his name from Salvatore to Charlie, and from Lucanis to Luciano, who once had survived such a brutal assassination attempt that forever after he would be known as "Lucky" Luciano. Lucky Luciano was proclaimed by *Time* magazine to be one of the most important figures of the twentieth century. Lucky Luciano downsized everything into workable order. He restructured, using Standard and Poor's stock ratings as much as he used Smith & Wesson guns to change the face of organized crime.

Born in Sicily in 1897, he relocated with his family to the lower east side of New York City when he was nine. He was a childhood friend of Al Capone, and he dropped out of school at the age of fourteen. He left his schooling behind him to hang out full-time on street corners. He and a bunch of other teenage Italian hoods had formed a gang they called the "Five-Pointers" and were soon regularly getting themselves arrested for shoplifting. It was while terrorizing local Jewish kids that he met one kid who stood up to him.

Meyer Suchowlański, a skinny Russian/Polish emigré five years his junior, refused to hand over any of his pocket money. Single-handedly, he simply defied the Five Points gang, and out of that bravado a lifelong friendship was born between the two of them. Within a few years the newly named Charlie Luciano and Meyer Lansky were mocking Prohibition laws by running whiskey from Canada into New York City. They teamed up with other thugs, notably Vito Genovese and Frank Costello, and in these two other gangsters they found men who shared their philosophy that doing business was more profitable than anything else that they would be doing. Lucky also brought into his inner circle the soon-to-be-famous "Bugsy" Siegel.

Lucky Luciano always marched to a different drummer than the rest of the world. In his personal life, he was not a family man. He was a bachelor who conducted his business out of a suite in the famous Waldorf Astoria hotel in central New York City.

Luciano came up with a way to solidify his personal power by holding the crime world's first "authentic convention" at the Blackstone Hotel in Chicago. There, Luciano offered up his vision of a united "national crime syndicate." He wanted to divide the United States and Canada into twenty-four regions and oversee the regions with a ruling commission. Seven men would sit on a board of directors made up of the bosses of each of the five New York families plus the bosses of the much smaller Buffalo and Chicago mobs. They would arbitrate disputes, set broad policy and establish a workable code of honor that reflected life in America.

For instance, only the commission could approve an

assassination to enforce the council's mandates, with a crew of killers controlled for them by Albert Anastasia that later became famous under the name of Murder, Incorporated. The wide-open western states such as Nevada and California were to become open territory, and the families could move in and out as evidenced by the recently departed Leonardo Da Vinci, who was working out of Los Angeles as an independent.

Da Vinci was gone, but there were plans for his replacement, and that is why the meeting was called. They needed to talk about setting up a new group of "made men" in the Los Angeles area, among other items.

CHAPTER TWO

Major crime is no longer bound by borders. Internationally organized crime gangs have formed alliances not unlike those of the corporate world itself.

These "unholy" alliances provide criminal groups with more power, more leverage, and more ill-gotten gains. These crime gangs are more formidable and dangerous than ever, and international law enforcement agencies have just begun the immense task of opposing them head-on and combating them.

§

It took mankind many thousands of years to move faster than the speed of a galloping horse. It then took less than a century to move faster than the speed of a train. From there it was only a few decades to move faster than the speed of sound. Today, satellites, cell phones, the internet and e-mail enable us to send our voice, our images, our ideas and our money out at the speed of light.

Our planet has been reduced to the size of a computer screen, and the artificial borders which we once called nations have, for all intents and purposes, begun to evaporate. We are now living through the greatest quantum leap in technology since Man invented the wheel. Radical changes in transportation and communication have allowed governments the ability to exercise controls over the movement of goods, services, people and ideas.

Here in the 1980s, we have witnessed both the concluding stages of globalization of markets and the initial stages of the globalization of crime. For much of the years following World War II, Italian organized crime syndicates became in practice and in fact the state itself. The Mafia's political power was derived directly from the enormous mass of money it was able to launder.

I want to put great emphasis on the word *launder* that I just used. To "launder," in this case, means to clean up or transform dirty money into clean. Once it becomes clean, it can be basically re-invested into everyday criminal activities.

The Mafia uses its money to hand out bribes and to accumulate profit. These criminal organizations have placed themselves into our political systems, and the Mob stands as an absolute model of pure "corporate efficiency."

This is a terrible model that has been replicated throughout the entire world. To achieve its goals, the underworld needs the upper world, which is made up of everyone and everything not connected to organized crime. Without the professionals such as lawyers, bankers, accountants and company formation agents to prepare the stage for global criminals, they could never function on the world market as successfully as they do. And yet, if there were not so much money to be made in worldwide crime, there would not be professionals to accommodate them.

Law enforcement as we know it today must be the local remedy to local problems. It is a statement of independence as represented by each individual government, and therefore by definition confined within the borders of each country. It is the individual countries that must tell their citizens that they may not perform illegal actions within their borders.

It is also the state that must pay the police to enforce the law and punish those who do not comply. Payment to police may not come from any private source other than the state itself.

My conclusion is that as long as we live in a world where the 17th-century philosophy of border enforcements is protected with an 18th-century model of open borders, then the 21st century will belong to transnational criminals and the rest of us will not have a chance.

CHAPTER THREE

Recently promoted Captain Charlie Glass of the Los Angeles County Sheriff's Office was carefully holding the allowed speed limit as he passed by the huge sign that indicated the end of the state of California and the beginning of the state of Nevada

Charlie had taken advantage of the many vacation days that he had coming from the Sheriff's Department and had decided to spend his time in the still-wild and untamed state of Nevada in order to unwind and get himself mentally ready to get back into the never-ending pressure of his office in L.A.

He needed gas, and so he pulled into the Shell station on the right side of the road. While the tank was filling up, he went into the men's room and washed up, after emptying his bladder of the five cups of coffee that he had consumed in order to stay awake during the five-hour drive from L.A.

As he returned to his car, he paused for a moment to read another huge overhead sign that welcomed him to the city of Stateline, Nevada, a gambler's paradise where "almost" anything goes.

Charlie had taken his time on his drive into Nevada as he enjoyed the peace and quiet of the roadside wilderness that was all around him. He was pleased to watch the wild animals whose path he drove past, as they dashed along, living out their lives.

Charlie had recently encountered human beings who were

wilder than those that he called animals, and he wondered about the future of the human race. At least when an animal became violent, it was because they were either hungry or competing for a mate. Humans just seemed to be violent for the very sake of violence itself.

He was getting headaches thinking about all these things and decided that he needed a vacation away from everyone and everything—and that included the love of his life, Sweetpea Soll. Sweetpea had sent him off and on his way with a big hug, a kiss, and the greatest smile that he had ever known.

He had left Los Angeles early that morning and had driven for the five hours that the trip took him to cross the California-Nevada state line. He stopped at the first gas station he saw, which was just across the border, and filled up his gas tank while he washed up and used the men's room.

He was hungry and ordered a breakfast special at a local coffee shop in one of the three hotels that he saw standing right next to each other. While he was waiting for his food to arrive, he picked up an advertisement from an open display box labeled "All the Things You Need to Know about Stateline, Nevada."

Having nothing better to do for the next few minutes, he read the paperwork and then folded it up for future reference and put it into the pocket of his jacket.

> Primm, or Stateline, as it is often called, is an unincorporated community in Clark County, Nevada, United States of America. It is noted primarily for its position, which straddles Interstate Highway I-15 where it crosses the border between California and northern Nevada.
>
> The community's economy is based upon its three casinos, which attract gamblers from southern California wanting to stop and freshen up before

going on to Las Vegas, which is about another 45-minute drive. Most of Primm's residents are employees of the casinos.

The last census listed the population of Primm as 436, with many thousands of tourists passing through the area on a daily basis.

There are 3 major casino hotels: Whiskey Pete's, Buffalo Bill's, and Primm
Valley Resort. There is one other very famous dance hall called the State Line Bar and Grill, located about three miles down the interstate on the way to Las Vegas.

They advertise that their way of doing business is unique, different, and has never been done before.

After reading about the "unique, different, and has never been done before" bar and grill, Charlie decided to stop by. He was looking for some laughs and diversions from his everyday hectic schedule.

Within the hour, he walked into the State Line Bar and Grill and from the first moment he stepped through the swinging doors and into the saloon itself, he had the feeling of simple elegance.

CHAPTER FOUR

The first thing that caught his eye was the gigantic mirror that was divided into four equal sections and stretched the entire length of the long bar. The high ceiling was filled with hanging lamps that gave a glow to the highly polished walls that reflected the brightness back into the large room. The floor was fitted, polished wood, and from the tops of the high oval windows, long drapes just barely kissed the floor. It was an elegant look, and it made him think of some of the stories he had heard about old-time Paris, France.

The next to the last feature of the room that most impressed him were the tables scattered about the room. They were made of hand-crafted heavy oak, padded in the seat and the back areas in soft colors that added to the overall feeling of relaxation that the travelers were supposed to feel when they arrived at the end of their journey.

The final touch to all of the things that impressed so much were the girls who were working behind the bar.

Charlie was pretty much an expert on girls who worked the saloons for a living. Inside the many saloons that he had visited either as an officer of the law or just as a private citizen, he had come in contact with the rough-and-ready types, the soft and fluffy, and the sweet, down-home-Texas kind of girl who just wanted to have a drink with you and take you to their bed for a fee.

Charlie loved to love them all and was always pleased to be with them and laugh with them. But this collection of Nevada girls seemed to be different. He was beginning to think that there was possibly something special about Nevada. He was beginning to think that maybe this was the place he was always looking for and could never find. It was going to be interesting to find out.

But in the meantime, he needed to take a good look at the girls. It had been a long time since he had been with a woman beside Sweetpea, and he missed having the good times that they always provided.

First of all, he had to get used to the fact that all six of the bartenders were female. Not one man was in sight except for the two gents who were standing on the second-floor landings looking down on everything. Their job was to make sure that everyone conducted themselves in a proper manner. They looked pretty nasty, and Charlie thought that their looks alone should keep the peace.

Charlie walked up to the section of the bar that had a perky blonde serving drinks from her exclusive section of the long bar. She looked to be in her early twenties, about five foot five or six, very slim of body with a great set of breasts that were very well displayed. Charlie, like most men, liked his women to be tall, slim, young and big-busted.

The interesting thing, when he looked carefully at the blonde behind the bar, was that the other girls who were also serving drinks could have been her twins. They were all dressed exactly the same, and physically they had the same bodies. The only difference was that his first choice was a blonde, and he also saw a redhead, a brunette, a strawberry blonde and a pitch-black-haired one. The effect was amazing, and he saw that he was not the only guy in the room looking at the bartenders.

Behind each girl on the glass mirror was a hand-printed cardboard sign that gave the girl's name and said in big letters that she was available if the price offered for her services was generous enough. It was a well-known fact that prostitution was perfectly legal in the State of Nevada.

Charlie, who was raised up in California where such a thing was illegal, had never seen anything like that advertised in such an open and out-there manner. This seemed to be a good thing in that it allowed the buyers to look over what exactly the young ladies were selling before they had to make an offer.

It seemed to be working pretty well, as new girls kept coming out of the back room to replace the girls who were serving drinks at the bar. Obviously, they had made an agreement with their customer, and they stepped away from the bar and led the gentleman up the rear stairs to where they probably went to fulfill their promises.

Charlie's girl of interest had her name of Sunny posted on the mirror. It seemed to fit her blond hair and great smile. Like all the other girls, she was well-dressed in a low-cut, semi-party dress that showed off her legs and breasts to great advantage. Charlie was mighty interested, and he made what he thought was a fair offer for her services, but she turned the offer down.

Being turned down was a big surprise. Charlie thought that $100 would lock up the deal That was the going rate in Los Angeles whenever he made a prostitution bust.

Charlie discussed the fee back and forth with Sunny for a little while, and since she looked so good and he had visions of sexy stuff dancing in his head, he accepted paying her the inflated price of $200 for her time. Charlie was thinking that she had better be the world's greatest lay for such a big expense. Charlie did not say that out loud, but he was thinking that.

Sunny, his new and most favorite bartender, had a great smile on her face, and a wiggle to her body that moved her large breasts in such a way that he almost jumped over the bar to grab hold of them.

Sunny was saying that the saloon was short two girls on her shift for the evening, and that she would not be relieved from serving drinks for about another hour. She hoped that the delay would not kill the agreement that we had made.

She asked again if I wanted to wait for her. If I did, she promised that I would not be sorry. Besides, she said that I was "cute."

Now I *have* been called "rugged" or "big." I gave her one of my best "cute" smiles. I took a parting look at her, pleased with knowing that I had made a good deal, and left the bar area and went into the large side room where I saw a lot of people sitting down in chairs so they could listen to someone who was about to speak.

I looked at the advertisement on the board outside the room and decided that this would be a good way to spend the time waiting on Sunny to finish up at the bar. The printed sign said that the speaker was someone named Nathan, who was the great-grandson of an eyewitness to the hottest story ever told, about a Wild West shootout called the gunfight at the O. K. Corral!

I squeezed into a corner and waited patiently for Nathan to appear. I wanted to hear all about Wyatt Earp and Doc Holliday and all the goings-on at the O. K. Coral, but my mind was still stuck on those great-looking breasts of Sunny the bartender.

CHAPTER FIVE

One of the two watchers who usually stood on the second level above the saloon floor passed out some paperwork that gave the background to what we were going to be hearing in a few minutes. I took the time to read it through. The papers read as follows:

OCTOBER 26, 1881—
TOMBSTONE, ARIZONA
TERRITORY OF THE UNITED STATES OF AMERICA

§

There was little that my great-grandfather, Nathan, whom I am named after, could do but watch as the feuding factions came together in a vacant lot between McDonald's assay office and C. S. Fly's lodging house. The vacant lot between the two buildings was the property of the O. K. Corral company, which used the area to board some of the local horses that were used by the Wells-Fargo stagecoach line.

My great-grandfather Nathan, who worked as a clerk at Johnson's assay office, was sitting on the front porch smoking a cigar on his lunch hour when all the gathering players started moving into the wide-open area of the corral. Great-grandfather Nathan immediately left the porch and went up to the second floor and stood by the open window looking down. He was close enough to see everything clearly and to hear their voices.

What he told our family was that he saw two groups of cowboys standing about twenty feet from each other. Great-grandfather knew all of them by sight, having lived in Tombstone his whole life.

The first group was made up of five men, two pairs of whom were brothers. They were the brothers Ike and Billy Clanton, the brothers McLaury, and Billy Clairborne, who was also known as a gunfighter.

The other group of four that was facing them were United States Marshal Wyatt Earp, and his two brothers, Virgil and Morgan Earp. Wyatt's friend, the infamous Doc Holliday who was known as a gunfighter, was also there.

Great-grandfather knew that there were bad feelings between the two groups. It was a known fact that the first group, made up of Clantons, McLaurys and Clairbourne, was known to be cattle rustlers and highwaymen. He also knew that the marshal's group had sworn to enforce the law and stop their "evil doings."

Both groups had completely avoided each other until they all came together at that moment when my great-grandfather Nathan was physically right there, on the spot, so to speak, to witness the goings-on.

Grandfather said that he saw that all four of the Earp group were wearing badges, and he assumed that Wyatt Earp, the marshal, had made them all his deputies for the round-up of the criminals that they were about to face down.

Everyone was armed with a six-shooter except for Tom McLaury, who stood behind his horse with a Winchester rifle on his saddle. He also noted that Doc Holliday, who was standing opposite Tom McLaury and his horse, had his pistol holstered at his side and held a sawed-off shotgun in his right hand.

Wyatt Earp was the first to speak and Great-grandfather heard his words loud and clear.

"All right, you sons of bitches, you've been looking for a fight, and now you can have it. Either drop your weapons or come up shooting".

"No!" shouted Ike Clanton. "Look, I'm not armed." He opened up his coat and showed that he was not carrying a gun.

"Up with your hands, now!" was Virgil Earp's reply.

Then things started happening much too fast for grandfather to see what started the shooting.

All at once, he saw Morgan Earp shoot Bill Clanton in the chest, while Wyatt, with a quick draw of his six-shooter, pumped three quick shots into Frank McLaury's stomach.

Great-grandfather said that he next heard Wyatt Earp yelling something weird that he was able to make out over all the noise and gunfire.

Wyatt Earp was yelling, "The fighting has now commenced. Fight or die."

Doc holiday fired both barrels of his shotgun directly into the other McLaury brother and then drew his six-shooter and began to fire.

Billy Clanton, as he was falling from a fatal gunshot wound, fired two quick shots, one hitting Morgan Earp and the other hitting Virgil Earp.

Great-grandfather Nathan thought that the entire shooting had taken less than sixty seconds and could not believe his watch when he took the time to look at it.

The totals from the shootings were both McLaury brothers and Billy Clanton dead, with the other two outlaws wounded. Doc Holliday, Virgil Earp and Morgan Earp were slightly wounded and only needed minor medical attention.

Of all the nine men who took part in the shoot-out, only Wyatt Earp was unhurt. He later said it was because of his living such a clean life. Everyone who heard him say that, laughed out loud and it was said that the loudest laughter of all was from Wyatt Earp himself.

The hero of this written report, Great-grandfather Nathan, got on his horse and took off for places far away. He realized that he was the only eyewitness to what had happened, and he knew that if he gave testimony, one group or the other would kill him, depending on what he said.

Great-grandfather Nathan headed off to California to stay with a sister. He thought that it would be much better for his health in the long run.

The management of State Line Bar and Grill thanks you for taking the time to read this article.

The great-grandson of the original Nathan will be speaking soon.

Sincerely
The management

§

Author Bud's sidebar notes and follow-up to the famous gunfight at the O.K. Corral:

With revenge as the absolute motive, the following events were put in motion and happened shortly thereafter:

Six months later, Morgan Earp was playing a game of pool with his brother Wyatt, when two masked men burst in and fired at the two brothers. Morgan Earp was killed, but the bullet meant for Wyatt completely missed and he went on with his life.

Three months after Morgan was killed, Virgil Earp was shot in the back with a shotgun blast. He died at the scene.

CHAPTER SIX

Charlie went back into the saloon area, where he received a wave from Sunny, who was just taking off her apron and handing it to the new girl coming on duty.

It was simply amazing how much the backup bartender looked like Sunny. The biggest difference, of course, was their hair color. Sunny was a blonde, and the other pretty lady had hair that was more into the brown shades.

Sunny pointed to a nearby table, and then pointed to the ladies' rest room. She wanted to freshen up a bit. When Sunny finally did come over and sit down, she brought with her a bottle of the house's finest wine and two glasses for them. She also said that she had taken the liberty of ordering them steaks for dinner. She said that she was absolutely starving because she wasn't able to take a break from the double shift that she had to work behind the bar.

Charlie was pleased to share the wine with her, and he said that he was also hungry. This would give him time to talk with Sunny and get to know who she really was besides being a bar girl.

While great-grandson Nathan's lecture was going on in the next room, they pretty much had the entire saloon area to themselves. The other bartenders, seeing that Sunny was with a paying customer, also left them alone. Dinner finally arrived, and their conversation was at a minimum as they each quickly put away the food that was placed before them.

Of course, her real name was not Sunny. That was just the professional name that she used when she was working. He learned that her given name was Barbara Jean, and that her friends called her Barb or Barbara.

She was twenty-seven years old, and came from a family of four sisters. She was the second to the youngest. They had lost their parents to sickness many years ago, and they had to split up and go their separate ways in order to survive.

She found herself to be good at bartending, and since they allowed her to do sexual encounters whenever she wanted, she found herself making a very good living. She just had to split her tips for services rendered on a fifty-fifty basis with the owners. That was why her fees were so high. This made a lot of good sense to Charlie, who knew all about doing whatever was needed to survive.

Sunny told him that her plans were to find the man of her dreams, get married, and raise lots of kids. She thought that, since she was so good at getting along with people, her future might be in owning a dress shop somewhere in a small town. She loved Nevada, where the weather was usually pleasant, and the people were more considerate than elsewhere.

They seemed to really enjoy talking to each other, but when they finally ran out of small talk, Sunny excused herself and said that she wanted to make herself more presentable for him. She gave him a key to the room she had reserved for the night. It was on the second floor toward the end of the long hallway. The room number was 234.

Charlie sat there and watched her as that magnificent body walked off toward the stairway that led to their room. He waited the proper amount of time, used the men's room off of the saloon floor, and then walked up the stairs that led to room 234.

§

At the feel of her hands on him, Charlie wrapped his arms around her and drew her against him. It was heavenly feeling her warm feminine body pressed up against him.

Her hands glided up to his cheeks, cupping them gently in her palms. She tipped her head up and gazed into his eyes with what he took for a longing that accelerated his heartbeat.

She settled her mouth on his with great precision, while her arms slid around his neck and her lips moved under his lips, which were soft and giving. Her tongue speared gently into his mouth, and he murmured his approval.

He pulled her tighter to his body, feeling a tide of desire wash over him. Her magnificent breasts pressed against his chest as he felt his excitement growing by leaps and bounds. His groin tightened in direct response to her, and he felt himself beginning to expand his manhood.

He knew that he was responding to her body far too quickly. With all of his self-discipline, his experience, and his willpower, he should have been able to delay a final erection for hours, and yet this special woman had him hungering for her even in the few minutes that they have been together.

He knew that he would be thinking about this day with Sunny, probably for the rest of his life! A life that he knew would be spent with his Sweetpea. That was a given. Sweetpea was absolutely wonderful and the girl that he knew he would ultimately marry. But until that time, as long as he was single and young enough to still be lustful, then doing what he was doing seemed proper in his mind.

And now, here he was with Sunny, but things were going along too fast for him to get full enjoyment out of it. Sunny was simply overwhelming him with her beauty and her willingness to be had by him. Her soft touch continued to quiver its way through him.

She snuggled closer, her hands gliding down his chest, around his waist, and then cupping his buttocks.

In turn, his fingers caressed along the low neckline of her blouse, then dipped into the fabric in order to release the first button that was holding it all together. He released the next button, then the next, thrilling her senses along with his.

Sunny did not expect a man as big as Charlie to be so tender and careful with her. His touch was absolutely soft and delicate, and she appreciated the soft approach he was taking. Finally her blouse gaped open, and he lifted it over her shoulders and dropped it to the floor in a heap.

He stroked gently along the edging of her bra, then between her breasts. He released the front clasp and reverently drew the restraining cups aside. The look of awe on his face nearly melted her heart. He was so sensitive, and she was rapidly learning to really appreciate him.

"You are exquisite!" he exclaimed.

His heated gaze took in her breasts, and her nipples puckered shamelessly. She longed for him to touch them, but he did not. He merely took in the sight of them as he finally unzipped the rest of her outfit and slid it down her hips.

She stepped out of it, now wearing only her pink ankle socks and skimpy black panties.

He hooked his fingers under the lacy elastic and drew them down, then off.

Now naked, except for her little pink socks, she felt alluring and yet somehow innocent. She felt like she was the schoolgirl that she had been only a few years ago. He seemed to bring out these good feelings within her; and she liked what she was seeing in this most interesting man who called himself Charlie.

He gazed down at the socks and smiled, as if he was having the same thoughts.

She took his hand and led him across the living room and into that section that was acting as the bedroom. The king-sized bed seemed appropriate for him. She was thinking that a tall and well-put-together man needed a big bed. She rolled the navy and forest green covers down to reveal cream-colored sheets and pillowcases with a fancy navy ribbon edging around them. She sat down, and the high-quality cotton sheets felt like silk against her naked skin.

Charlie tossed aside two of the pillows and moved the remaining two to the center of the bed. "Why don't you lie on your stomach, Sunny?" he suggested.

CHAPTER SEVEN

Sunny settled onto her stomach, tucking one pillow under her chin and pushing the other aside.

He sat down beside her, and his hands began moving over her back in long soothing strokes. Relaxing, rhythmic circles up the center of her back, across her shoulders, then down to her hips, then up the center once again.

She found herself relaxing under his sure touch. She thought that she was supposed to be giving him pleasure, but here he was doing wonderful things to her instead. It seemed to make him happy just touching her, and she was happy being touched in such a remarkable fashion.

He rolled her over onto her side, and moved her hands over her head. With one hand, he held her hands while they were still up above her head. With his free hand, he wandered over her well-formed and very firm breasts.

This was what he had been waiting for all afternoon. His free hand moved from one nipple to the other, and to Charlie, this special touching was well worth the high price he had to pay for the use of this very willing female body. Charlie was a happy man.

Charlie felt himself growing hard. He had always been a breast man, and this girl had the ultimate set. He was having one of the best times of his life as he pulled her flat onto her back once again. What a great vacation this was turning out to be!

As she rolled back and he released her hands, he grasped the pillow and repositioned it under her head. She just lay there, staring up at him, her body simply beautiful in its nakedness. Her breasts pointed straight up to the ceiling, the nipples fully erect. Her soft, golden pubic hair curled daintily between her thighs as her extremely long legs parted in anticipation of his entry.

He eased her legs further apart, and carefully positioned himself between them. He gently drew the folds leading to her womanhood apart and dabbed his tongue against the tender flesh that led into her inner chamber.

Sunny's fingers tangled in his thick black hair, and she moaned in pleasure from what he was beginning to do to her.

He took a moment and lifted his head up and just gazed down at her. She looked absolutely beautiful to him, and he gave the biggest of sighs, then nudged her thighs wider apart as the sweet smell of her urged him on and into an intoxicating series of moves. His eyes closed again as his head went back while he sucked in a lungful of air.

The engorged and swollen head of his huge erection pierced and at last finally entered the young lady. This was that special moment for him. This was probably the highlight of his sexual life up to that moment. He had never had a woman like Sunny in bed with him, and he was enjoying every single glorious moment of it.

Murder and mayhem were the last things on his mind as he pushed himself up and onto his elbows and, with his eyes closed, drilled deeper and deeper into her female depths. He was glorified in the feelings that the heavenly sliding of her body beneath him gave to him. He never wanted this wonderful moment to end, but he knew that it would.

All good and wonderful things always come to an end and this was no exception to that rule as the fire within him was raging to get loose. His need for release was too much for him, and as he was coming to his completion, he felt her getting caught up in that special moment with him.

Sunny was rocking back and forth as she matched his pounding motions with her own strong body. And finally, he stroked one final, mind-blowing stroke, and completed his act!

He was immediately followed by Sunny who screamed out loud with the ultimate pleasure that Charlie had just given her. It was the best screw she had ever had, and she let out a scream of pleasure that she was sure came from her toes on up to her head.

They both lay there panting next to each other, and just looking into each other's eyes. This was a special moment that they shared with each other and nothing could ever take away the memory of it for either of them for the rest of their lives.

Within moments, they both fell into a wonderfully deep sleep, completely entwined within each other's arms. The falling night's sounds around them were completely ignored as they slept on.

§

It was possibly three or four hours later when Sunny was awakened by Charlie's hands, which were gently moving around her breasts.

He felt the now-familiar rise of her nipples under his touch, and knew that she was ready for the next round of his lovemaking. Not a word was spoken between them as he gently but firmly rolled her over onto her stomach.

The woman was obviously well trained, and she immediately took up the proper position of putting her weight on her forward-leaning arms, and lifted up her rear end, with her legs nicely spread out.

The bright moonlight coming in through the window showed him a special picture that he was sure that he would never forget. Here was a fabulous female, on her hands and knees, with a great set of breasts hanging down and just waiting for him to fondle them.

She was starting to make some up-and-down motions in anticipation of his entering her from the rear, but he was not a fool and he was not in a hurry to do so. Moments like these were few and far between, and he wanted to drag them out for as long as he could.

He ran his hands over her swaying butt, and around those marvelous breasts once again. He was really enjoying himself tremendously, until his own erection got in his way. He knew that it was time to finish off his lovemaking with what was his favorite way of doing so. He reached forward and played with her breasts for the very last time. He would really miss them.

Charlie was a breast man, as are so many other males, and he did what they all would have done if they were lucky enough to be exactly where he was at that moment. He gave that great twosome one last squeeze and then entered Sunny from the rear.

He smiled when he heard her gasp as his huge erection went just where it belonged. She would remember for a long time why Charlie was called "Big Charlie."

He continued to pump into this willing woman, going deeper and deeper until he was in as far in as he could go. He felt her expanding and stretching internally as she took in all of him.

Minutes later, he was completely done, and he climbed off and held Sunny one last time, as they again spoke no words and fell asleep in each other's arms. These were moments to remember.

CHAPTER EIGHT

Newly appointed Captain Charlie Glass woke up with a start. It took him a few moments to focus on where he was. He quickly realized that he was back home, in his own bed, completely alone, where he had slept the sleep of the truly exhausted.

He slowly got himself up, took a long shower and followed that with a quick shave, got dressed and grabbed something boring from the refrigerator, and then headed out the door. He was planning on getting an early start to his job after his most wonderful and exciting vacation. He was ready to get back into the routine of his normal work cycle down at the Sheriff's headquarters.

He would always remember "Sunny," but she was just a passing fancy, and he knew that his heart belonged to Sweetpea.

Moving on from the thoughts of the women in his life was easier than he had thought it would be, once he walked into his new office at work. He looked at the backed-up paperwork on his desk and decided that everything could wait. He had to go downstairs into the lower level and see Beth Sherman. He took the stairs down to the commanding officer's clerical basement office, which was located in the very center of the first sub-basement.

Police officer Beth Sherman was there, sitting at her word processor, watching it print out a report. Beth was in civilian clothes and looked like the grandmother everybody wished they had. Beth was a good friend and one of Charlie's favorite people in the whole world.

She was delighted to see him and greeted him with a "Morning, Charlie! Glad to see you back from your vacation. It wasn't the same around here without you. Things were just too quiet without you here to stir things up like you always do. That was some job you did on the Da Vinci case. Too bad he had to die! He would have been a valuable asset."

"Morning, Beth. What are you doing here so early? I thought I was the only early bird."

"I'm not here early, Charlie. I'm here late, and it's all your fault! There is so much paperwork because of you and that exciting Da Vinci case of yours. I had to clean up all the details for you about Da Vinci and his organization. It is a crying shame that Joe would not let you take him in alive. He would have been worth his weight in gold for all the information he had bouncing around in that good-looking head of his.

"I've been working on this report of yours all night. It was such an interesting read that I just couldn't put it down. So I just stayed here and worked right through until now. I should be able to call it a day in an hour or so and then I'll head home to catch up on some sleep."

Charlie was thinking to himself, *Twenty hours straight and she's still ticking without a complaint. She is the best.*

Beth had been in the Sheriff's department for over thirty years. She had joined the department in the days when women were restricted to the roles of cell matrons at the downtown jail. Rumor had it that she had left a very high-paying job as a legal secretary with a big law firm to join the Sheriff's Department, and the "job" quickly became her life.

Beth was competent to the point of boredom. She was considered the authority in the department on what form had to be filled out in any situation, or what obscure office procedure had to be reviewed in connection with a special case, and so on. As the years went by, her protégées, using the lessons they had learned from her, rose rapidly within the department, and they all remembered how they had gotten to where they were. She was the most sought-after clerical Sheriff's officer in her entire department.

The printer stopped, and Beth tore the pages from the machine and gave them to Charlie. She got up, stretched for a moment and smiled up at him. "I'm going out to breakfast and to freshen myself up a bit. Be sure you are gone and that private report is in my in-basket when you leave. I just wanted you to see what was in the official report when I had finished with it."

She smiled, kissed Charlie on the cheek, opened the door and left him alone with the report.

§

Thirty minutes later, a still-smiling Charlie was upstairs sitting at his desk.

The official report that he had just read had made him out to be some sort of law enforcement genius! It went into extreme detail upon how he had found, isolated and destroyed Da Vinci and his Organized Crime Network within the greater Los Angeles area. The report that he carefully put into Beth's in-basket made him look absolutely great. He could not be more pleased.

He spent the next few minutes on the telephone with David Mark himself, from the best florist in town, Designs by David. David, as always, was very helpful with his suggestions, and Charlie ended up ordering the biggest and most expensive bouquet of flowers with a special two-pound box of chocolates to be sent to Beth Sherman forthwith.

Charlie sat there quietly for a few minutes trying to calm himself down as he watched both Joe Wahl and Roberto Sanchez doing paperwork at their desks in their adjacent offices. He told himself that everything around him was going to be just business as usual, but in the back of his mind he knew that he still had to deal with the problem of the mole that had infiltrated his department. Mole, mole, who was the mole?

CHAPTER NINE

Charlie knew that he needed a new face in the department that he was heading up. It had to be someone he could trust completely, and whose integrity and trustworthiness were beyond question. He loved both Joe and Roberto, but because of the overhanging problem of the mole, he was really not comfortable working that closely with them right now, as he would have to be if he made one of them his number-two guy.

Before he did any more thinking about all his personal problems, he took a moment to call Sweetpea and make a dinner date for them for tomorrow night, which would be a Tuesday. Tuesday nights in L.A. were usually slow nights for most restaurants, and they didn't have to make reservations. They could just walk into most places and not have to wait to be seated and served.

After hanging up with the love of his life, Charlie was able to concentrate on how to organize his new Department of Special and High-Profile Crimes, and he came to what he thought were several wise decisions. He would have both Joe Wahl and Roberto Sanchez assigned as lead commanders on different casebooks. In this way, they would both be comfortable being in complete charge of an important case of their own.

It also meant that Charlie would not have to meet up with either of them except when they would all get together once a month to talk about their case updates and hear what the others were doing. This once-a-month-meeting was Charlie's idea, and he was hopeful that an exchange of insights into each other's cases would be helpful.

After putting his Joe Wahl and Roberto Sanchez problem to bed for the moment, he still had to decide who his new number-two backup was going to be. He thought that it would be an intelligent idea on his part to pick Danny Ossen for the position.

Danny was one of the most knowledgeable and highly respected detectives in the Sheriff's Detective Bureau, and one of Charlie's best friends from years past. They had worked well together on many cases in the L.A. Robbery Squad and in the Career Criminal Apprehension Unit. The buzz going around at that time was that Glass and Ossen were a first-rate team, and they did get great results on the cases that they had worked together.

Last year Danny Ossen had retired from the Sheriff's Department with close to thirty-five years of service on his record. But retirement didn't agree with him! He missed the "bright lights," and he missed all the action that came along with the job. So Danny had come back to the job, and he was assigned to clerking duties on the major case squad. It was not exciting, but it kept his hand in.

Charlie finally located Danny filling out a chair in the squad coffee room. *He's starting to show his years,* Charlie was thinking as he walked across the room to where he was sitting. He was also losing some of his hair and showing some wrinkles, but he still looked great to Charlie, who had a real liking for the man.

Danny looked up from his coffee as Charlie pulled up a chair and sat down next to him. "Hi, kid. It looks like you're the new man of the hour around here! Closing that Da Vinci case gave you the front page on all the newspapers. I was holding two copies of the local papers for you. I thought you might want one for your scrapbook and one for you to read. I knew that you took off on your vacation before those papers hit the streets." Danny rose from his chair, and the two friends shook hands and then sat down again.

A smiling Charlie asked his soon-to-be number two, "Am I good news or bad news in all those papers you've been reading?"

"Mostly good, Charlie. These tabloids love those police-shootout stories, as long as only the bad guys or the cops get hit."

CHAPTER TEN

If a hotel can be called grand, imposing, opulent and majestic, then surely the Hotel de Paris deserves those descriptive adjectives and more. One would be hard-pressed to find its match anywhere in the world, and yet this world-class hotel is right here in Beverly Hills.

The hotel restaurant was named for King Louis XV, who reigned in France from 1710 to 1774. It is decorated in the extravagant and most exaggerated rococo style that defined the period of his rule.

Approaching it from the outside, one is confronted with a downsized exact replica of the Eiffel Tower, an eye-catcher done up in the colors of the French flag, which waves at the world just inside the doorway.

Into the wide, beautifully paved and landscaped front driveway, a specially made black Mercedes model E55 touring car rolled up, and Charlie could be seen handing the keys to the doorman as he walked around the front of the car to help his young lady slide out of the massive passenger seat that she seemed to have hopelessly sunk into.

For the evening dinner out with Charlie, Sweetpea had decided to wear a pair of camel-colored leggings that hugged her slim legs like a glove. Her boots were three-inch camel leather that came just above her knees and accentuated her lovely legs. A long-sleeved red V-neck sweater set off her beautiful black hair nicely;

she wore it in a simple ponytail pulled back and held by a few sparkling hair clips.

She could not help but notice that the innermost interior of the beautiful hotel's dining room was ringed with groupings of ornate arches showing off painted embracing cupids, supported by twenty-four square marble columns. The tables were far apart and the food and services absolutely impeccable! The restaurant's own bakery provided a variety of over twenty-nine different kinds of breads and rolls. Sweetpea knew that she was in for a culinary treat if—with all the many distractions going on about them—she could still pay attention to the food being served.

As expected, the meal was fantastic and met both of their high expectations. Each of them was perfectly content just to sit there quietly enjoying each other's company as they slowly sipped their imported Italian wine.

Sweetpea was thinking to herself that this would be a perfect moment to ask Charlie to explain some things that she still did not understand about their Sheriff's Department's crackdown on crime in the county of Los Angeles.

Even though she had read carefully every single memo and report that came across her desk in the Sheriff's Legal Department where she worked every day, she still wasn't sure that she understood just what it was that Charlie and the deputies were actually doing. Without her understanding fully where the Department was heading, she felt uncomfortable, and hoped that Charlie would be able to give her a greater understanding of what it was that they were dealing with.

Charlie acknowledged her question as being a good one and paused for a moment or two as he considered his answer. He knew that Sweetpea was well aware of how the Department worked and he knew that he could jump right into the small bits of information that she was not familiar with. He told her that he would have go back a number of years to when L.A. was still feeling the pressure of having many of the "boys" from the eastern Mafia gangs walking around openly in the streets and doing their business without respecting anyone who got in their way.

Charlie looked deeply into the eyes of the girl he loved, took a sip or two of the delicious wine that they were sharing and then began a brief summary of the street criminal facts that he knew Sweetpea needed to understand.

The usual types of hoodlums who came to Los Angeles from back east did not care what anyone said about them. For them, it was always business as usual, and the hell with anything else. This was true up to the late 1970s and early '80s. Beginning around this time, the Sheriff's Department and the LAPD began to detect a major shift in the nationwide underworld activities and how the underworld went about doing things.

The racket bosses back east had decided to go "respectable." They wanted to fit in with the rest of society and not stand out as misfits anymore. Quite openly, by using front men or "stooges" as we call them, the Mob in Los Angeles had orders to invest heavily in wholesale and retail legitimate businesses. The thought was to give themselves an upright appearance, and not have their business dealings stand out from the crowd as they had in past years where everyone watched every move they made.

Publicity was a killer to them. It was ruinous to their image, and the Sheriff's Department, in cooperation with the LAPD, kept exposing their known activities upon every news media possible. We were hoping that exposure on television and in the newspapers and magazines would keep the out-of-towners and the casual racketeers away, and the policy began to succeed immediately and handsomely for a while.

In the ten years before the LAPD and the Sheriff's Department put their heads together and came up with this working plan, there had been eight gangland killings, all being in the Chicago style, which was very bloody and very heavy-handed. In every one of these older cases, promising suspects were arrested, but they all were turned loose to go back on the streets because they all had air-tight alibis. Against this type of underworld activity and cover-up, both the sheriff and LAPD were powerless.

Then finally, in the late '70s, the intelligence divisions for both crime-fighting agencies shifted their tactics and went into a successful attack mode against organized crime. Instead of the futile "pinch-them-and-sweat-them" tactics of the past, thirty-seven detectives from both agencies combined their efforts and went about collecting every scrap of evidence about the workings of organized crime in their jurisdictions.

This new approach that was based upon how the United States armed forces did their investigations. Now they would gather information upon each known crime member before they were arrested, and when they were taken into custody, their criminal files and how they went about doing the bad things that they were doing were already prepared and ready to go against them.

They did not have to start from scratch with each arrest. Things started to move along at a rapid pace, and before the attorneys for the crime syndicate could move for dismissal, formal charges were made and the bad guys would spend time in jail until their case came up in the court system, which was always a long time.

There were suddenly more arrests—and a greater need for prison holding cells for the arrested felons who were awaiting court hearings than there was room. All possible holding locations in and around the city and its neighborhoods were full to the brim, and with the criminal-organization men off the streets, the crime level in the cities had a sudden drop. The policing agencies knew they were on the right path when only a trickle of new "made men" would come into the city, where there used to be a flood of them.

There were very special qualifications needed for these law enforcement officers. They had to be immune to temptation from the crime syndicates, and they had to be able to step into and out of the different parts of the city at a moment's notice. The plan was to have new detective faces coming and going before they could be tempted with offers from the bad guys. This rotation system kept new faces constantly showing up and the detectives would not become comfortable with the men they were watching and arresting. These detectives had to be close-mouthed, because the security of the entire operation would rest on each one of them working together with no outside interference from the bad guys.

As with any subversive elements, the battle against them was being run by highly trained intelligence agents who would operate as one huge unit with centrally control of the gathered factual information.

To get things off the ground and running smoothly, they checked hundreds of sources that dealt exclusively with the "Who's Who of crime" within the known boundaries of the United States. Thousands of details gave up personal histories within the backgrounds and the connections that these criminals had carved out for themselves over the years. An amazing amount of information was readily available to the investigators. There were many names of other known associates who were also "bad guys" according to the many laws that they were constantly breaking. There were also lists of where they lived, whom they associated with, the names of their businesses and names of family members, and information from other law-enforcement agencies, local and out-of-town newspapers and personal police notes with ongoing activities included.

With so much "hot" information flowing into the downtown Sheriff's jail facility, a special floor safe made up of heavy steel and always under guard twenty-four hours a day was created and overviewed directly by the Los Angeles Sheriff's department.

Many other approaches were available to the Sheriff's newly appointed intelligence officers, who were instructed to continue with their efforts in pushing the prevention of big and organized crime within the city. These intelligence workers saw to it that the word got out to the other cities around the country, that L.A. was from that point on to be considered a dangerous place for the crime syndicates to operate in.

And locally, on a day-to-day schedule, detectives would follow known criminals as they made their rounds of the city. The detectives never talked to the people that they followed, but made themselves noticed. The idea was to make everyone associated with these "known men" uncomfortable, knowing that they were being watched. But before they would be able to get rid of these low-level mobsters, something had to be done about the boys at the top of the criminal organizations.

Tony Brancato and Tony Trombino were two of the most well-known and troubling pair of criminals running around openly in the city. They were both from Kansas City; when they saw how wide-open Los Angeles was, they moved all of their activities into the area. The two "Tonys" were just one level under the heads of the local bosses, but they were patient and ambitious, and they knew that it was just a matter of time until they moved up the local criminal ladder of success.

At this time, Tony Brancato had been able to get himself out of jail by posting a cash bond that clearly noted that he was involved within the courts as he fought extradition from Los Angeles back to Las Vegas. His wanted posters called him a prime suspect in a $35,000 stickup at the Las Vegas Flamingo casino. The LAPD and the Sheriff's Department had him as their number-one suspect for the killing of four local people, and the FBI listed him on its Ten Most Wanted criminals list.

The other Tony, Trombino by name, had a long record of holdups, muscle jobs and narcotics connections. He had just gotten out of prison some two months ago when a witness suddenly disappeared. Without the witness, the case quickly was thrown out, and Tony Trombino was free once again to walk the streets.

Trombino's wife had made a special dinner for her two "Tonys" on a Tuesday night. After having eaten their fill, they told Mrs. "T" that they were going to take a ride and get some air. Later that evening, probably around eight o'clock, they stopped by a friend's apartment and picked him up to join them for drinks at a local bar.

This special friend must have been someone of importance in the organization, because he was allowed to sit in the back seat all by himself. This put him directly behind the two Tonys, who were seated in the front seats. They parked the car on a hilly Hollywood street that looked down upon the famous Sunset Strip in Hollywood, where they parked and talked. The police reports that were later filed assumed that the conversation was most likely about money to cover the two Tonys' much-needed bail money.

However, and it was a shocking error on the part of the two Tonys, the friend in the back seat turned out not to be a friend after all. From his position in the back seat of the car, he pulled out a .38-caliber pistol and calmly put two bullets into the back of Trombino's head. A third bullet was also found in his shoulder.

The other Tony most likely was too stunned by the noise of the gun, and it appeared he did not make any moves to defend himself from the rear-seat shooter. He immediately caught the next bullet in the center of the back of his head. Pieces of brain tissue were found splattered all over the front seats. The shooter immediately fled the scene of the crime and was never found.

It was only a few hours until the Sheriff's Department finished with the crime scene and was able to send out searchers for the murderer. The groupings of detectives were changed every six hours in order to keep the investigation moving.

For the next ten days, the LAPD and the Sheriff's Department shook up the local underworld from top to bottom as they looked for the killer. Grifters, local muscle guys, businessmen, party girls and Hollywood bit-movie players were all questioned and re-questioned, but nothing of interest came up. A total of five local gamblers and hoodlums were arrested and booked into the local jail.

The LAPD and the Sheriff's Department checked out every possible lead as they searched all of the two Tonys' hangouts. Nothing of any real interest ever came up.

Even with all of the resources of the two departments, nothing ever was learned about the killing. And even with the tremendous power of the Los Angeles County grand jury behind the investigation, nothing was ever discovered.

The Mafia and its organization had everyone who might have known something afraid to speak up. The criminal code of silence stood in the way of justice. Even friends and family of these two crime victims could or would not accept help from the law.

The word out on the street were common words that were used all the time in connection with crimes of this sort: *il dimenticato ritornerà* (the forgotten will return)—and spoken words will cause more death.

It was a known fact that some Mafia boss somewhere back East had set forth the death notice against the two Tonys, and that was the end of the matter. It is a well-known fact that the two Tonys never knew about their death sentences that had been handed down from back east.

With the two Tonys sentenced without their knowledge, a local Mafia "shooter" was told what had to be done. It was this unknown person who carried out the Mafia "justice."

The main suspect in the "two Tonys" murder case was "Jimmy the Weasel" Fratiano, who had a reputation on the streets as the local Mafia's enforcer. The records showed that a few days before the violent death of the two Tonys happened, it was Jimmy the Weasel who had taken them both to lunch at one of the local

Hollywood restaurants. His alibi was very weak for the day and time involved in the shootings, but nothing ever came up that would stop Jimmy the Weasel from walking away as a free man.

Even though the evidence against him would not hold up, he was put on a "watch sheet" and constantly followed wherever he went. The patience of law enforcement finally paid off. Jimmy the Weasel, a few months later, tried to move in on a famous local development company. He was actually recorded as making a death threat to one of the partners if he did not give up his shares of ownership in his company to them.

The intended victim gave his consent, and the Sheriff's Department made three tape recordings of the "Weasel's" conversations, which had death threats on them. In strong and obscene words, Jimmy the Weasel made many demands and warned everyone that if they did not do as he ordered, then the people back east who he worked for would come after them.

The Weasel was shortly sent to San Quentin Prison after being found guilty of the charge of extortion against others. The Mob back east got the message and left the area to stay put and concentrate upon areas that they could control. To our knowledge, the Mob has not returned in any great numbers out west.

"And here, Sweetpea, is the focal point that I am trying to make for you. With organized crime pulled out of the entire West Coast, a vacuum suddenly existed, and into it stepped smaller and much more devious independent operators from the local gangs who make their living selling drugs on the streets.

Our problem here in the Los Angeles area is no longer organized crime. Our problem is the independents and the violent street gangs who moved into the areas that were left unattended by the mobsters.

The war on crime has now pretty much changed from threats of bodily harm to problems created by easily available street drugs from South America and Mexico. Our war on physical crime is now a war on drugs and the tremendous power and money being made off the trade."

There was a pause in the conversation as Charlie continued to sip at his wine and Sweetpea thought about all the things he had told her.

She nodded to herself, realizing that she better get much more acquainted with her computer and see what she could learn about the drug trade that Charlie said was going on all around them. She knew she needed to get a better knowledge of what Charlie was dealing with if she wanted to keep his interest.

CHAPTER ELEVEN

The heavy driving rain was unrelenting, whipped into a complete frenzy by the howling winds as the waves surged and crashed against the coastline of the Southern California shore.

In the shallow waters just offshore, a dozen or so dark figures bobbed, clinging to their buoyant, waterproof haversacks like survivors of a shipwreck. The freak storm had caught the men completely unawares, but it was a good thing. The storm provided better cover for their illegal landing than they could have hoped for.

From the beach, a pinpoint of red light flashed on and off twice, a signal from the advance team that it was safe to land. "Safe." What did that mean?

Tossed and buffeted about by the heaving swells, the men made their way toward the beach, and in one coordinated move, clambered silently onto the sand. Stripping off their black rubber dry suits to reveal dark clothing and blackened faces, they removed their weapons from their haversacks and began distributing their arsenal. Heckler and Koch MP10 submachine guns, Kalashnikovs and sniper rifles were their weapons of choice.

The twelve sealed boxes of narcotics that they had secretly smuggled into Southern California from Mexico were dragged up to the waiting truck that would take the boxes and their guards to a quiet hideaway where they would rest up and wait for their marching orders. Everything that they would be doing was precisely orchestrated by the man from Central Mexico who had trained them so exhaustively, and so tirelessly for the last few months.

§

About twenty-five miles away from the shoreline of the Santa Monica beach, where the landing was quietly taking place, there was a high-level meeting going on in the penthouse of one of downtown Los Angeles's high-rise buildings. This was a special meeting called for by newly appointed Sheriff's Department Captain Charlie Glass that was supposed to address two important and completely different events.

Charlie had quietly worked behind the scenes to achieve the special appointments that were being celebrated this evening: the transfer of his former partner, Joe Wahl, into the lead position of commander of the newly formed Sheriff's Department Drug Enforcement Division, and the special assignment for Roberto Sanchez to the Sheriff's Department FBI coordinating bureau, to be located in the FBI's downtown headquarters.

This was the only way that Charlie could remove both men from having eyes and ears within his own comings and goings. With them out of the way of his day-to-day load, Charlie hoped to work with his new number two, Danny Ossen, on cases that would come up on the usual daily basis, and yet, at the same time they could watch both Joe and Roberto for any underworld connection that might pop up, allowing them to finally nail down who was the "rat" he knew was in the Sheriff's Department.

The second part of the evening's events was a special report by an FBI expert upon the Crips and Bloods gangs that were now filling the void left by the almost complete disappearance of organized crime from the Los Angeles County area. The evening was winding down a bit as Charlie turned over the microphone to the FBI speaker for the evening. He returned to the central table and joined Sweetpea, Danny Ossen, Joe Wahl and Roberto Sanchez as they all turned their attention to the special speaker.

The speaker introduced himself as Joseph Meyers. He looked very serious as he took out his notes and moved to the center of the speaker's platform, where he picked up the microphone and began to speak in a strong but pleasant tone of voice. "Thank you all for allowing me to be here to share a few thoughts with you on behalf of the FBI."

I have been asked by the director to thank everyone at the Los Angeles Sheriff's Department and the Los Angeles Police Department for a job well done on driving out the criminal elements of that criminal organization commonly known as the Mafia from the Southern California area.

We have confirmed from all of our many sources that you have successfully forced these criminals out from your area, and that is a wonderful thing. However, when they left, they left an empty space, and it only took a few months for that vacuum to be filled up again with elements of society that are just as bad, if not worse, than those whom you ran out of town. The biggest problem that the state of California is now facing is the tremendous increase in the size and the strength of the local street gangs.

These are not out-of-state people. These are people who were born and raised in and around the Los Angeles area. They live here with their friends and relatives and are a part of our community. The problem with these friends and neighbors who are known to all of us is that instead of going out and getting jobs like the majority of the locals have done, many of our friends and neighbors have joined the local gang culture where they deal in drugs, guns, prostitution, and anything illegal.

Gangs have been a part of our society for hundreds of years, and today, here in the 1980s, they are bigger and more dangerous than at any time before. The gang origins lie in lack of education, general poverty and racism. Black and Latino gangs here in Los Angeles originally started as a protective response to white racism, but they quickly spun out of control.

Prior to the late 1970s, there were many black and Latino youths who were looking for an outlet to satisfy their anger with the problems that surrounded them on all sides. The quiet times changed in California due to the fact that the black and Latino populations doubled in size as people came here to work.

The community, with its rapid growth and industries, offered many jobs that were labor-intensive. However, in the late 1970s blacks and Latinos were restricted to where they could live, especially here in southern California. They had to live along the edges of the downtown areas, mostly on the east side of the city. Huntington Beach, Bell, South Gate, Inglewood, Compton, Gardena and West Los Angeles all had white gangs that would seek out blacks and Latinos and harass them or beat them up if they ventured out of the areas normally associated with their daily living.

The first black and Latino gangs that were formed were strictly for protection. These gangs, however, were almost exclusively focused on territory, and the crime rates began to soar. The beginnings of the narcotic inflow only worsened the effect, as the local gangs increased their membership by the hundreds and spread out of the local neighborhoods into the entire state of California and then into the rest of the country.

As the influence of gangs spiraled out of control with the now-introduced drug trade, a truce among the various gangs went into effect, and the gangs were no longer fighting among themselves because there was enough territory and cash flow to keep almost everyone happy. Due to a general truce among local gangs here in 1980, there has been a decline in the number of gang-related deaths.

The LAPD and the Sheriff's Department focused on the gang problem, and many gang members found themselves in jail. Today, as I speak, the gangs are still out there and are very active. They still offer their members a sense of family or the belonging that was missing in their lives. However, it has come at a price.

All these gangs have had a destructive effect on their local communities. They have quite often torn their local areas apart rather than uplifted them in any way. And it is the local newspapers and news media that continue to create an image of gang members as heroes and survivors as they glorify them. But most people that have been touched by gang violence in their own personal lives know that there are very few positive things that come out of having gangs moving about openly in their communities.

And now, if you will allow me, I will conclude with a brief explanation of how the local gangs began and how they are still going.

The Crips organization was founded by Raymond Washington and Stanley Williams in Los Angeles in 1969, and it is still operating today. The Crips are made up mostly of African Americans with a membership somewhere between 30,000 and 35,000 members. The Crips gang activities are basically drug traffic, robbery, extortion, murder, burglary, prostitution, and theft. Other gang associates are the Folk Nation, Gangster Disciples, La Roza Nation, Black Guerilla Family and the Juggalos. Gang rivals to the Crips are the Bloods, People Nation and the Ñetas.

What once was a simple alliance between two autonomous gangs, the Bloods and the Crips, has changed over time into open warfare that is pitting one gang against the other in their fight for territory and drug distribution. By 1978 there were forty-five different Crips gangs walking the streets of Los Angeles. Several local leaders were taken off the street by 1980, and this broke up the gangs into small compact groups that operated independently of each other but still shared similar goals.

It was the introduction of crack cocaine that put the gangs back together as a united grouping. There was plenty of drug money for everyone and all the parts of the Crips gangs were able to work together again. It was only with the Bloods that they continued to have problems. These huge profits from the distribution of drugs induced many Crip gangs to establish personal markets in other cities of the United States.

An interesting side bar on the name of Crips is that their original name was "Cribs," as in a baby playpen. This was to show that their first members were very young, mostly age 17. The name was later changed to "Crips" and it has never changed again.

The Crips are always involved in looking for new gang members to add to their numbers and thereby to their strength. Presently there are over 800 sets, or mini-gangs, that make up the Los Angeles Crips, with over 13,000 active members out of the 35,000 nationwide groups who use the name. The three states with the highest estimated number of "Crip sets" are California, Florida, and Illinois. Lately the almost exclusively black membership has allowed whites, Hispanic and Asian men into its membership.

After a few current years of peace between them, a major feud began between the Piru Street Boys and the other Crips. It quickly turned violent as gang warfare ensued between these former allies. The battle continued, and in 1981 the Piru Street Boys wanted to end the useless violence. They called for a meeting with all the various Crips gangs.

After a long and very unsuccessful series of meetings, the Piru Street Boys broke off all connections with the Crips groups and started a brand-new organization that would soon be calling themselves the "Bloods." The Bloods quickly grew into a major-sized gang and soon became the main rivals to the Crips. The rivalry between the Bloods and the Crips would grow tremendously, and accounted for most of the gang-related murders that were happening in south central Los Angeles.

In the early 1980s, as many gang members of both the Bloods and the Crips were being sent to various prisons across the country, a new alliance was formed in the jails between Crip members and the Folk Nation. This mostly happened in the Midwest and Southern states.

This alliance, which still exists today, is strong inside the prisons, but is less effective once gang members get released from jail and get back out there on the streets. The alliance between the Crips and the Folk Nation is known as "8-ball."

§

And finally a quick note on the "Bloods": the Bloods are a primarily, although not exclusively African American street gang that was founded in Los Angeles. The gang is widely known for its rivalry with the Crips, who wear blue colors to identify themselves from the Bloods, whose colors are various shades of red. Each gang, beside wearing their special colors, uses distinctive hand signals to identify themselves to others.

The Bloods broke up into small groups within the coverage of the larger gang, which call themselves "blood sets." Presently, in our early 1980s, there are fifteen Blood groups or active sets, but the Crips still outnumber them 3 to 1 in membership.

Since their creation, the Bloods have also branched themselves out across the entire United States. Bloods have very strong representation in the United States military, and are found in strong numbers in overseas bases.

Once again it must be pointed out that the rivalry between Bloods and Crips dates back to the 1960s when Raymond Washington and seven other Crips members confronted Sylvester Scott and Benson Owen, who were young students at Centennial High School in the city of Compton. In response to this attack, Scott, who lived in Compton, started the Piru Street Boys, which later became the first Bloods gang.

In order to establish a reputation of their own, the Bloods soon became the more violent of the two groups. In the early 1980s the Bloods are leading the way in the very profitable distribution of cocaine that is constantly being smuggled into the United States through California.

Blood members also identify themselves to each other by red clothing, symbols, tattoos, jewelry, graffiti, language and specific hand signs. Most Bloods wear team jackets which clearly show off the red gang colors. One of the favorite blood symbols seems to be a five-pointed star.

This five-pointed star is to show their connection to the "People Nation," another large and very influential gang that is quite often in and out of the prison system also.

"Thank you for your attention." The FBI speaker stepped down and took his seat.

CHAPTER TWELVE

Danny Ossen had worked as a Sheriff's deputy for thirty-one years, and after a big retirement party, he had cut off all of his ties with the Sheriff's Department and retired to the easy life of fishing and backpacking with a group of other single male friends.

The problem for Danny was that he was getting bored with his retirement. He missed the sometime violence provided by the job, and the companionship of other "cops," whose brotherhood was like no other. And so, after two years of trying the civilian life, he had decided that he missed the action that being involved in the many Sheriff's investigations provided him, and re-enlisted for another go-around.

He was hoping to get back to active duty, but as the Captain had explained to him, the department had decided to go with a younger guy to fill his old position. After all, they said, he was now in his early fifties, and his reaction time to an emergency situation would not be the same as it was when he started with the department. And so, in order to just get back into "the job," he had accepted the desk that was offered to him. He was just grateful and happy to be back into the old routine.

All of this changed when he was asked out to lunch by his old friend Charlie Glass, who was a rapidly rising star within the department. Charlie's claim to fame came with his very successful conclusion of the Da Vinci case, with the crime family being run out of L.A. and the death of Da Vinci himself.

In the old days when they both were just breaking into the department, they had worked well together, and they were able to take down some of the big names in the crime syndicate that was working the Los Angeles area at that time. Danny was not sure if the lunch date was "a welcome back to the department" lunch or something else that Charlie had on his mind. Charlie was never known as someone who would waste his time with idle conversation, and so Danny's curiosity was fully up and running, hoping that Charlie had something in mind that he could do beside sitting behind a desk.

Danny had never been to the old and established restaurant called Musso and Frank, which was located just west of the central downtown area. Charlie had checked both of their work schedules and saw that they were off the duty roster for this Saturday, and not being on company time gave them the leisure for their upcoming lunch.

Danny was right on time as he pulled into the large frontal area, where he handed off his car to the waiting parking attendant. The exterior of the restaurant was nothing special and consisted of a blackish colored set of exterior walls with the name Russo & Frank in large letters and smaller letters beneath the title stating that they served the finest in Italian Cuisine.

When he stepped into the restaurant's interior, the surrounding completely changed for the better. The walls were a soft gold and white, a background to many of the mounted pictures showing off the wonderful cities of Italy, with other famous Italian scenes in evidence.

As he was led to the table where he saw Charlie Glass already seated, his eyes roamed about the tastefully decorated walls and the elegant black-and-white tablecloths that set off the silver and white table settings.

Noting that his escort was also dressed in an elegant black and white jacket and tie, Danny was glad that he himself was wearing a tie and jacket. Danny also noted that the table where Charlie was sitting was the last in a long row of wonderfully displayed tables with only a huge window behind him and few if any nearby tables that would allow someone to listen in on their conversation.

Danny understood from the location being far from the beaten path that this was not going to be a social visit, but one of Charlie's famous informal business lunches. Danny was getting excited, but nothing showed in his manner or greeting as he and Charlie exchanged a manly bear hug before they sat down.

After the usual small talk, Charlie steered the conversation back to business at the Sheriff's Department and told Danny that he could use him on a very prominent and important case that had come across his desk within the last few days.

It seemed that with the disappearance of the Italian crime families from the city that there was a vacuum created in the game of "Sex for Sale," and it had become a million-dollar industry.

The problem that the LAPD and the Sheriff's Department had was that everyone working for their departments, by law, had to have their picture and identification posted on their employee lists within a ninety-day period of being hired. The list gave open access to anyone who wished to find this information. Only the very recently hired people were not yet listed, and thereby they remained invisible to the "bad guys" who might be looking at the file.

Charlie said that there was a very specific investigation going on that needed somebody with a great deal of experience in all sorts of private investigations who might want to jump in and take over. That someone absolutely could not be on the ninety-day-plus list, and Charlie's investigation into the availability of someone who had the experience and qualifications was limited to just one name, and that guy was Danny Ossen, a veteran of many years, whose file had been closed down when he retired and was taken off of all lists. The fact that Danny Ossen was re-hired less than ninety days before their luncheon date made him the perfect pick to run the investigation that Charlie had in mind. Charlie pulled out a thick white envelope and handed it to Danny, who was sitting across the table from him.

With a great big smile and a firm nod of his head, Danny indicated that he was very interested, and that he would like to read the information that Charlie obviously had for him.

Charlie sipped very slowly at his drink and settled back in his chair as he watched Danny open the envelope, smooth out the folded pages and begin to read. Charlie could not but help notice the twinkle in Danny's eyes as he was thinking that this could be his step back into doing something important for the Sheriff's Department once again.

Danny straightened out the papers and silently began to read the report.

§

Her name was Rita Rose and she was well known as the madam to the stars of Hollywood and beyond.

Rita Rose had lawyers who advised her how to avoid getting into trouble with the law. They had a complete list that was updated daily with the names, history and pictures of every male and female police person on the LAPD and the Sheriff's Department roster of employees. These pictures and descriptions were posted at her offices in Beverly Hills and at different locations wherever she had her girls working.

Every client that was seen by the group was screened first by Rita herself, who was very careful whom she allowed to use the various services that her company offered. Rita was known to also get personally involved with her "clients" if the price was right, and she was known to keep a special "little black book" with all the names and numbers of everyone who had used her services.

Rita knew that the only way she could get in trouble was to be caught red-handed, so to speak, so she went beyond a normal screening by telephone and met with potential clients for coffee. For many years Rita and her girls were always one step ahead of the law and could always turn away from a trap by referring to the list of police faces on the up-to-the-moment list that she always kept.

The status quo remained unchanged until one day, Charlie Glass came up with the idea of using someone fresh and new to the posted lists that Rita would have a copy of. He knew that he needed an experienced but fresh face who would know how to gather the needed evidence and did not appear on Rita's picture-book of law-enforcement officers.

§

Danny Ossen closed the file, smiled and shook the hand of his superior officer and friend. They had a deal that would bring the famous Hollywood Madam to justice.

CHAPTER THIRTEEN

Before we disclose how Rita Rose was "busted" for running a prostitution ring, allow us a moment to talk about a few interesting things that came out of her arrest.

When she was arrested and charged with running a high-class prostitution business in Los Angeles, California, the "Hollywood Madam" refused to release any of the names in her famous little black book that was full of names and telephone numbers to the rich and famous.

One check to her was made out for $53,000. Added to the evidence was a handwritten note from the sheriff's jail booking clerk.

It said, and I quote: "I would like to know what kind of service Rita or one of her girls could provide for one night that was worth $53,000?"

§

SIDEBAR OF INFORMATION ON Rita Rose

Rita Rose was born in Los Angeles, California on December 30,1965. After dropping out of high school, she launched a high-class prostitution ring that would cater to only the very rich and very famous as well as other high-end clients. She was very pleased when she found out that she was being referred to around the Los Angeles area as "the Hollywood madam to the stars"!

She was arrested by means of a well-thought-out plot hatched by Detective Charlie Glass of the Los Angeles Sheriff's Department. The department was able to overcome the well-thought-out defenses that she had built around herself.

§

The details of this famous arrest will follow shortly.

§

Rita, when arrested and forever after, refused to reveal the information from her famous little black book that had all the names and telephone numbers of her famous and infamous (there were some highly placed criminal names mixed in there) clients, according to reports that came out many years later. This little black book became famous for what everyone thought was in it, but the public and the opposing lawyers never were able to get their hands on it. The book was referred to many times at the several trials that Rita had to endure, and the book itself did not come up until many years later, when it was auctioned off for a large sum. This little black book and its author, Rita Rose, became so famous that three movies were based on it, and it made the producers a lot of money.

After much delay and much court theatrics by Rita's lawyers, she was finally sentenced to three years in prison.

Rita Rose was one of six children born to a very prominent pediatrician. She dropped out of high school at the age of sixteen. She did get a high school equivalency diploma several years later, but had sent in someone else to sign her name and sit in on the required classes for her.

At the age of seventeen, she got a job as a local waitress, and by accident met Barry Cornblum, an illegal money manager who had a great influence on her life. It was Barry who introduced her to Elizabeth Adams, a longtime Beverly Hills madam who dealt exclusively with wealthy clients.

In the middle 1980s, Rita launched her own high-class prostitution ring, based upon what she learned from Elizabeth Adams and with the money backing she needed from Barry Cornblum. It was only a few years until she earned and kept the title of the "Hollywood madam to the stars."

After being arrested and booked by the Sheriff's Department, which will be detailed following this interesting background information on Rita, she received a mandatory minimum sentence of three years in prison. But her attorney, who received tremendous fees for his services, had her conviction overturned, and she was once again a free woman who returned to her old habits.

But this did not last long! The following year she was arrested again, this time not by the State of California, but by the federal government, which went after her for income tax evasion and money laundering. These new charges stuck; she was found guilty of all charges of money laundering, and she spent thirty-seven months at the Federal Correctional Institution in Dublin, California.

Once again, her trial drew extensive media news coverage, as it was speculated that she now would reveal the names in her now-famous little black book in return for a lighter sentence. Rita refused the offer of less jail time if she would reveal the names of her clients. She refused to do so and served her full jail time as required by law.

Many famous and not-so-famous people were thrilled by her courageous action, which they believed was a great example of doing the right thing. At prison she constantly received gifts of food baskets and flowers, which she shared with her fellow inmates. This made her very popular both at the prison and in the newspapers, that were keeping track of the former "madam to the stars".

Finally, it has been estimated that Rita Rose successfully hid from the government five million dollars, which she had waiting for her when she finished up her full sentence of thirty-seven months in the federal prison system.

And now, here is how she was carefully and correctly arrested by the California law enforcement officials who, under the guidance of Charlie Glass, made the case for the State of California.

CHAPTER FOURTEEN

Before the meeting with Charlie Glass broke up, Danny Ossen was given an 8½ x 11 manila file folder that was completely sealed and had written on it the words "for Danny Ossen's eyes only." Danny agreed to read whatever was inside of the folder right away, and would be ready for the meeting that Charlie told him was scheduled in his office for Monday morning at eleven o'clock.

Another bear hug and a "Goodbye" sent Danny on his way to his apartment with a spring in his step that he knew had been missing for the past many months. Hopefully the contents of the file would get him back into the "game," and he was all excited about that as he finally sat down at the small work desk located in one of the comers of his large apartment.

When he had gone into retirement from the Sheriff's Department, he was given his pension funding in a lump sum, and with it, Danny had bought a high-rise apartment on Wilshire Boulevard, which was a very exclusive West Los Angeles neighborhood. He was on the twentieth floor of the building, and that gave him a clear and un-obstructed view of the famous Westwood campus of UCLA.

He cleared off the few papers that he had on his work desk and carefully opened the sealed manila folder. He took out all the papers from the folder and turned on the reading lamp that would shine down upon whatever it was that he was looking at.

The letterhead was that of the Sheriff's Department, with the notation that it was from the desk of Charlie Glass. Danny began to read through the thick pile of papers.

§

Hi, Danny:

Here is some background on the case that I would like you to get involved in. You will be working as a single investigator on this, and you will be reporting directly to me. The case heading will be "Rita Rose" and the full support of the Sheriff's Department will be available to you if things go bad.

Rita Rose, as you must know, is called the "madam to the stars" and the sheriff himself has asked us to clean up this black mark against our city. We are talking about prostitution, which is the business of engaging in sexual activity in exchange for payment or some other sort of benefit.

Prostitution laws make it a crime in most states—and that includes California—for anyone to offer, agree to or engage in a sexual act for compensation. The only exception in the western United States is the state of Nevada, which has legalized prostitution with some loose controls on all activities.

A female who works in this field is called a prostitute and is considered as a sort of sex worker. It is often referred to as the world's oldest profession, and recent estimates place the annual revenue generated worldwide as well over $100 billion dollars. Some of the names for women involved in this line of work are whore, hooker, call girl, business girl, b-girl, streetwalker, trollop, strumpet, courtesan, escort, lady of the evening, working girl, doxy, scarlet woman, harlot, etc., etc.

A funny story just came to mind as I was making out the above list for you. It has to do with the word "hooker," and it goes something like this:

§

The War between the States, or the Civil War as it is sometimes called, ended many years ago in 1865 with the final surrender of the South's General Robert E. Lee to the Northern general Ulysses S. Grant.

A year or so before the deciding big battles were to be fought that would end the four-year war, one of General Grant's commanders complained that many of his soldiers were coming and going out of their encampment each night. This was a terrible thing to be happening, because with the big battles coming up soon, the army needed to be at absolute full strength at all times.

This commander held an immediate investigation, and it provided him with the answer to his up-and-down manpower problems. It seems that his men were sneaking in and out of the camp in the middle of the night to visit the local prostitutes in the nearby city.

Now Commander Hooker could secure the camp so that no one could get in or out, or he could allow the women, or camp-followers, as he called them, to come into the camp and spend their nights there. He decided to let the ladies come and go as they pleased, and in that way, he would always know where his men would be when he needed them.

The system worked out so well that a new term was added to the local language. Girls who provided these services to the soldiers and came and went as they pleased became known as "General Hooker's girls."

In later years when the term became better known to the public at large, these girls became simply known as "hookers."

CHAPTER FIFTEEN

OK, Danny! I really hope that you enjoyed my little sidebar story. Let's get back to Rita Rose!

The only way that we are going to make any of our charges stick against her is to actually catch her in the act. This is a very hard thing to do, because she has pictures and records on everyone in the Sheriff's or LAPD files due to the new open-access laws.

If she is not personally involved in something, then it will be impossible to get any charges against her. Her high-priced attorney would easily get her off! The one thing that we have going for us is the known fact that she likes to get in bed with some of her wealthy clients.

How would you, Danny Ossen, like to be the guy to "stick it" to the Madam to the Stars and get paid for doing it? I just might be handing you the undercover job of the century, and you could retire and do the dinner-club tour for years and years.

So we are going to try a different approach this time to see if we can involve her in something of her own free will that will be usable in court, and this is exactly where you come in. As of yesterday morning, when I checked all personal files for our guys and the LAPD, I found out that your name has not been picked up for the public record yet. Your name will not appear for another thirty days, since you have been back with us only about two months. This means that you will be completely unknown when they check out your name against their records, and if we build up your background to that of a rich son-of-a-bitch who can afford Rita's personal fees, then we might get you into her playhouse.

I do realize that it is asking a lot of you to spend money like a millionaire and go to bed with a beautiful young woman who will probably tie up all your working parts into knots, but we would appreciate it if you would try it out.

I am assuming that you will accept this once-in-a-lifetime assignment, and I will need you to bring to our meeting on Monday some pictures on yourself playing golf or going to the beach while you were between jobs. We need to build up your playboy image for Rita's investigators, and we also need to put a lot of money into your private checking account.

Try not to let your imagination get the best of you—at least, until I see you on Monday.

As always, my very best regards,
Charlie Glass

§

Danny re-read the letter for a second time and just sat perfectly still for a little while.

Then, with a big smile on his face, he took the letter and placed it inside the open safe that seemed to be waiting for him. He spun the combination numbers, walked into the master bedroom, jumped into the shower, came out and went to sleep, where he expected to dream erotic dreams. Danny Ossen was a happy guy.

CHAPTER SIXTEEN

It wasn't until well past noon on Monday before Charlie and Danny were able to get together to discuss the Rita Rose case and a few other things. They ended up walking away from the Sheriff's Department downtown location and chatted away about everything except police matters.

It wasn't until they settled in at a Burger King that was not too far away from their offices that Charlie began to fill Danny in on what had been going on about the role that he was going to play in the planned takedown of Rita Rose.

An account had been opened up at a nearby City National Bank and would show a balance for the past two years at well over two hundred thousand dollars in his personal accounts. Danny was going to have a record of private investments that had made him into a rich man who could afford the services of all sorts of girls. He was to be known as a man about town who enjoyed the ladies but was not tied down to one. Danny was going to be recommended to the booking agent who handled Rita Rose's schedule from a known associate of her attorney who was looking for a favor in return.

Here was the problem, and it was a big one. Anyone who was accepted by Rita Rose as a temporary lover was carefully searched by the bodyguard who was always by her side. And if they were together in an intimate situation, he could not be wearing a recording device on his body. It would, of course, show up once his clothes were no longer being worn.

Another great big problem was that if Danny went to her office or other places of work that she controlled, there would be her cameras and her warning devices all over.

The solution was obvious. Take Rita out of her comfort zone and her usual locations where she was well protected and observed by those who worked for her.

It was Danny who suggested that somehow, he had to meet her in a normal situation where she would not know that he knew who and what she was. They needed to make a study of her habits as she went about her normal daily routine. Did she go to the theatre or the movies or perhaps a favorite and secure place to have a quiet drink with friends?

Charlie agreed to find out these things by use of some of the ways that the Sheriff's Department went about finding things out about a person of interest to them.

Danny's job was to get involved as a man-about-town who had nothing but time and lots of money. And the best way of all was to get friendly with a bodyguard of hers, or a hairdresser, or even go so far as bumping his car into hers and create a minor car accident where, if she was driving herself about town as she was known to do, they would have to exchange drivers' licenses and other information with each other. If he put on a good enough show, she would want to check out the information she took from him to give to her insurance company.

If she checked him out, and the odds said that she definitely would, she would find out that he had the money she required, was single and enjoyed a good time. He was the perfect potential client for her ever-expanding business.

The accident plan seemed to be the best way to make the introduction, and Charlie Glass had auto-theft boys follow her around town until a pattern emerged as to how she spent her time.

Once they knew her personal habits, Danny could make his move on her.

And the last piece of the puzzle was for Danny to take her out to dinner in a fine restaurant at the Beverly Hills Hotel where he would be staying in the penthouse. The penthouse would be completely under the video-taping eye of the Sheriff's Department, who would be there to catch her taking money from Danny as a client. At least, that was the plan.

CHAPTER SEVENTEEN

It was a warm July afternoon in Los Angeles, and Danny Ossen, dressed in a pair of jeans and matching gold-trimmed shirt, was patiently waiting for Rita to get back into her car after she left a jewelry store in a free-standing building in the farmer's market area of West Los Angeles.

Danny who had spent some ten days following her about as she went through her daily chores like marketing, the cleaners, etc., was waiting for the perfect moment to have his new, top-of-the-line BMW sports car make its contact with one of the fenders of the convertible that she was driving.

Rita Rose was an interesting young lady to look at. The records told him that she was in her middle twenties, and she seemed to prefer going her own way without her usual bodyguard, who was always with her during her working hours. If Danny had not known who she was, he would have assumed that she was just another very pretty girl who dressed very well and was probably trying to get herself into the movies.

She carried herself with a lot of poise and great posture. The Sheriff Department's readout on her said that she was five foot four, one hundred and eighteen pounds, and had a pretty face and a slim body with a great set of boobs.

Danny could not wait to make his move and get into bed with this Hollywood Madam who probably knew all the exciting sexual things that her rich and famous clients paid thousands of dollars to experience with her or one of her girls. As he watched her come out of the jewelry store carrying several small bags, she looked just like any other of the good-looking ladies who were all over Los Angeles. The difference with this specific charming one was that he was actually stalking her on behalf of the Sheriff's Department.

There were only two ways to exit the parking lot on La Brea Ave, and if she took the one where Danny was patiently sitting and waiting, then he would create the accident that he needed for his introduction. As luck would have it she took the correct exit, which would have taken her to one of the nearby freeways going into Beverly Hills.

The interesting thing about this exit was that it had a blind spot, and that if he played it right, she would not see him coming as he slid his car into position so that her left front fender would come in contact with his right fender. Timing was everything.

CHAPTER EIGHTEEN

The following series of events, names, dates, persons involved, conversations both direct and indirect, etc., were taken from the personal notes and experiences of Danny Ossen, acting as an undercover agent for the Los Angeles Sheriff's Department. The investigation is under the direct supervision of the Sheriff's Internal Investigation Division as set up by Charlie Glass #444-333-222.

All other evidence of the above investigation came from the tapes, both video and audio, made in the specially prepared penthouse of the Beverly Hills Hotel, located within the city of Beverly Hills, California. Reinforcement of the above audio and video evidence is confirmed by sheriff's deputy Danny Ossen and is entered into the record. The only thing edited out of the video tape was the actual physical and sexual encounter between Rita Rose and the undercover agent.

An important and quite obvious point must be stated here, and that is that in order to make the case against Rita Rose, there had to have occurred several closely connected sexual encounters between deputy and defendant.

§

The following information has been taken from the physical case file labeled Rita Rose. This is a copy of the first and original interview with undercover agent Danny Ossen, who was speaking for the official record. This report starts with the initial first contact made with the suspect and goes through the step-by-step moves that were made to gather enough physical evidence to take the case to court.

For the record, this is the official first recording and set-up file on the Rita Rose case as dictated by myself, Danny Ossen, the only person to come in contact with the female known as Rita Rose. I had been given the case by Senior Detective Charlie Glass, and we are now going through the process of putting together the necessary paperwork to present evidence for the court system.

I was told by the young man who is with me now while I am making this official recording to just talk to him as if he was a personal friend. I will be allowed to edit or change anything that I wish before the report goes up the chain of command.

And so, with a cup of coffee in front of me and some nibble food provided to me courtesy of Sweetpea from the front office, I hereby offer up my report.

CHAPTER NINETEEN

As previously stated, I waited in the parking lot of the Farmers Market in West Los Angeles.

Just as she was pulling out of the driveway and beginning to make a right-hand turn, I quickly put my car on a collision course with hers and was pleased when my right fender made a slight indentation upon her left front fender about a foot or two before her door.

I knew that at the rate of speed when our two cars bumped (which my speedometer told me was under five miles per hour) she would not be hurt, and I was pleased with that. I wanted to be very careful not to hurt or injure her in any manner.

After we had both pulled our cars off to the side of the street, we exchanged drivers' licenses, and I learned officially that her name was Rita Rose and she learned that my name was Danny Ossen. I accepted full responsibility for the accident and gave her my personal cell number to call after she talked to her insurance company.

I remarked that neither of us was wearing a wedding ring, and perhaps it was meant to be that we had met this way. I suggested that when she called me about the insurance, we could perhaps have a few laughs over a drink and get to know each other. She was pleasant and quite charming but not wanting to commit on the drinks part.

About a week went by, during which I spent the time working at my Sheriff's Department desk, when finally I received her call.

Her voice was so sweet that I thought her throat must be coated with honey as she told me that the estimate on her damage was eighteen hundred dollars and did I want to put it through my insurance company or cash.

I told her cash was preferred since I did not want such a small incident to cause my insurance rates to go up. I asked her for a dinner date so that I could give her my cashier's check and my sincere apology for putting her through all the trouble she had to go through to get the estimate.

Obviously, she had checked out my name and the information I gave her along with my driver's license number and learned that I was really a single, rich guy running around town. She quickly accepted my dinner-and-drinks offer and gave me her home address for me to pick her up Sunday evening. Sunday was the first time she would be free from work, and we made my pick-up time for her at six o'clock.

I told her I would make the dinner reservation and told her to dress up because we would be going to one of the better restaurants in Beverly Hills.

Her answer was positive, and we hung up with a warm good-by.

I was excited, and after about an hour or so, Charlie Glass walked into my office and sat down with a big sigh. I could tell he was tired and must have had a bad day. Perhaps my news would pick him up, which it did.

He told me to make the reservations at the Beverly Hills Hotel Steak House, and then see, after I told Rita that I was staying at the penthouse in that very same hotel, if I could get her to join me for an after-dinner drink in my room, which would be the "set-up" penthouse. Charlie and I went into further details, and he left with a smile on his face that he did not have when he came in.

§

Sunday night could not come fast enough for me, but finally there I was, standing outside her apartment door, which was on the seventh floor on Beverly Drive in Beverly Hills, a very expensive area.

As I stepped into the entry way of her fabulous-looking apartment, she took a moment out to give me a quick look around at all her amazing furnishings, and then we went down the elevator, across the huge lobby, and into the waiting cab.

She smiled deeply when I told her that she looked fabulous, and that I blessed the day that our two cars kissed outside the parking lot at Farmers Market. She laughed and kissed me on the cheek. I was almost sorry that the evening would hopefully end with an awful experience for her. She seemed beautiful, smart, and very sexy. The perfect woman with only one problem—and that was that her body was for sale when the price was right. Very sad.

The cab dropped us right in front of the lobby of the Beverly Hills Hotel, and within a few minutes we had passed through the beautiful lobby and were seated at the window table I had reserved for our dinner.

The view of the lights of Beverly Hills and Los Angeles were fantastic. The dinner was great, the service unbelievable, and the conversation interesting. She was asking me all sort of questions about how I earned a living, and I gave her all sorts of lies. I was learning to tell lies and make them believable. I could tell that she was taking in every word I said just as she was taking in almost a whole bottle of the finest wine the restaurant was able to serve us.

When the conversation turned around from me to her, she did not skip a beat as she told me about her hard life growing up in Los Angeles and not really going anywhere until she made friends with a lady friend who taught her how to make an easy dollar and have a wonderful time doing so.

Without any prompting on my end, she went into her life story of how she became a madam, and how once in a while, she would turn a trick or two if she really liked the guy—and if he could afford her rates, which were ten thousand dollars for the evening.

When I did not show surprise at what she was telling me, she went ahead and asked if I wanted to show her my apartment, which she knew was the penthouse here at the Beverly Wilshire Hotel. The only problem she had was that she needed cash in advance with a new client, and could he produce it?

I laughed and said that for the use of her body for the night it was a bargain at that price, and I said that I had that amount in my wall safe upstairs. No problem at all.

We swapped lies for a while as she continued to finish off the fine bottle of wine I had bought for her.

After I signed for the check and we left the restaurant, the self-service elevator was being held open by one of the bellhops for us.

As I finished pushing the button for the floor, she turned me around and gave me one long, passionate kiss that had us both gasping for breath. She said that the kiss was just a sample of what was in store for me once we got into the room.

The elevator stopped at the penthouse level, and as I opened the door she walked into the foyer. The room was most impressive not only to her but to myself, since I had only been here one time to practice opening the safe where the cash was waiting to complete the trap.

As we walked around and took in the full-circle-view windows, she kicked off her heels and asked to see the money before the evening went any further. She said that of course the first time was for money, but if I was as good as she thought it would be, the second time was her treat.

I gave her my best smile, went and opened the safe and took out a stack of one-hundred-dollar bills. I counted out the right amount, then put the rest back into the safe, which I carefully closed and locked.

As I was turning back from the wall safe, I saw her tuck the cash into her purse. I was hoping that the hidden camera had caught her moves, since it was the basic part of the case we were building against her.

She picked up her purse and the extra handbag she had carried with her all evening, and said she was going to freshen up and change into her "working clothes" in the bathroom, and would I please turn down the bed and the lights to just a pleasant glow. With a big smile on her face and a great wiggle in her walk, she walked into the bathroom and closed the door.

Even though I knew that I was on camera, I followed her directions to the letter.

I stripped off the covers from the huge double bed and turned down the lights just a little bit. I did not want the room to be too dark for the camera to catch the action, in case the pictures were needed for the court case.

CHAPTER TWENTY

Now all that I had to do was wait, I reviewed in my mind if there was anything at all that I had to do to complete my end of the operation.

We already had the evidence of Rita taking the money from me and putting it into her purse. When she came out of the bathroom, the video would catch her in whatever sexy outfit she would be wearing, and as soon as I put my arms around her, thereby making physical contact, the requirements for her arrest and the following charges would definitely be met.

Now I was perfectly fine meeting all the legal requirements to make a good case against her, but on a personal level I was not satisfied if I ended things here without satisfying myself. I worked long and hard to get things to where they now were, and I strongly believed that hard work deserves to be rewarded. I decided that I would stay and play with the highly desirable Rita Rose.

After all, her time was paid for, and she had agreed to perform the proper services that the payment called for. Even if I was an undercover cop, a deal is a deal. For ten thousand dollars, I should have the greatest bed-time I could ever want from the famed "madam to the stars."

After I had turned down the lights and the bed, I took off all of my clothing except for my shorts. I took a position on the end of the bed so that I could watch Rita exit the bathroom. I had

96

expected her to open the door and step out into the bedroom where I was sitting, all dressed up in something skimpy. Well, she fooled me, and I was glad to be the fool.

She was absolutely exquisite and she knew it as she stepped forward a few steps and made a very slow circle so that I could clearly see all of her. She knew that I would be admiring her thin little bra that caused her perfectly sized breasts to push up and out as they called out to me. The rest of her skimpy but absolutely magnificent outfit consisted of tiny bikini-sized panties, black stockings held up by a matching black garter belt, and the highest pair of high heels I had ever seen.

In her hand she was carrying a small tape recorder, and with the biggest of smiles on her pretty face, she pushed the play button and out came a soft version of a "bump-and-grind" song that one would expect to hear at a burlesque show.

Now if I had had the time, I would have slowed everything down so as to make it last for maybe a half hour or more, but I knew that I was being recorded. I would have loved to have stayed and played with the ten-thousand-dollar lady, but the circumstances were all against me. So instead of sitting back and letting her make wild passionate love to me like I am sure she usually did for all of her clients, I completely surprised her.

Right in the middle of one of her bump-and-grind moves, I stood up, moved behind her and unhooked the bra, and with a quick move removed her panties. I left her stockings on as well as the shoes. I thought they would look good in the video when I reviewed it with the boys down at the-sheriff's station.

Without saying a word to her, I stepped out of my shorts, picked her up and walked over to the bed, where I placed her face-down on the mattress.

This position was probably not uncommon for her because without saying a word she took up the right position for me to enter her from the rear. She put her arms in front of her head and drew up her knees so that her rear end was up and ready for me to enter.

I was in somewhat of a hurry, but not so much of a hurry that I couldn't slow down and reach forward to play with her full and wonderful breasts.

After I satisfied myself there, I pushed the cheeks of her butt farther apart and entered her from the rear. I was sure that she had sex in this position many times, but I had a smile on my face as I heard her make all the proper noises as I had my way with her.

It wasn't long until I came to a climax, and either she was faking one or she was a great actress, as she too seemed to be finished up. I did not wait for the usual conversation that would follow our wonderful sex act. I forcefully rolled her over onto her back, and without any fore-play whatsoever, I entered her in the standard position.

She surprised me by getting into the game as she did. Her great enthusiasm almost overwhelmed me as she gave matching movements to every push and grind that I plunged into her. If I was a paying customer, I would definitely believe that I had gotten my money's worth.

In a few minutes we both lay on our backs and tried to catch our breath. She finally got up on one elbow, leaned over and kissed my cheek and then gathered up her clothing that was all over the room.

I felt like a real bad guy as I quickly put on my clothing and closed the door behind me. I knew that the boys shooting the videos would come down to the room, wait for her to come out of the bathroom and then place her under arrest. Even though I knew it was part of my job as an undercover agent to do something like this, I did not feel good about how it all came down.

I went home, took a hot shower and went to sleep.

Many weeks later, I learned from Charlie that with her attorney doing some great moves, she walked away from all charges brought against her by the city of Los Angeles.

However justice, slow as it was in coming, finally caught up with Rita Rose when she was convicted of income-tax evasion. It appears that she "forgot" to report any and all cash that she had received for her services. I heard that she was sentenced to thirty-seven months in jail.

For me, life went back to the old routine.

CHAPTER TWENTY-ONE

Ellen Burchett was very much younger than Charlie had expected and very attractive. She was dressed in a slim-lined beige suit with a silk blouse to match, which was open at the neck to reveal three striking gold chains. A cloud of fluffy, streaked blond hair drifted to her shoulders, and she had a way of tossing her head to send it flying back around her bright and animated face.

She greeted Charlie with a warm smile and extended a perfectly manicured hand. "Hi, you must be Detective Charlie Glass. That is a fantastic name."

"Thank you," said Charlie.

Ellen gestured to one of the gray tweed sofas that was set off against one wall of the postage-stamp-sized office. "Please sit down," she said, as she moved from behind her desk to join him.

Charlie sat and looked around the room.

Ellen's solid black desk was stacked with papers, scripts, and photos of actors, which were all over her desk and on the coffee table in front of the couch. A bulletin board on the wall near the desk was overflowing with schedules, messages, scrapes of paper on which were scribbled reminders, phone numbers, a *TV Guide* cover, and a few personal snapshots. The overall effect was definitely one of complete chaos.

But this was merely a cover for one of the most brilliant minds working undercover for the United States Customs division of the federal government. Ellen was able to speak and understand the written and spoken dialects of Spanish as spoken with the accent of a different style unique to the Mexican Cartel, and not to the rest of the Spanish-speaking world.

As Ellen sat down next to Charlie on the sofa, she handed him a handwritten piece of paper and pointed at him and then at the letter.

Charlie understood that she wanted him to read the note immediately, which he did.

> *Charlie, this room is definitely bugged and we have a lot to talk about, so it would be best if you asked me out for lunch at one of the nearby local eating places.*
>
> *Be sure that you say that you were recommended to see me about the kitchen set you are thinking about getting for your house.*
>
> *Also, be sure to mention the name of our so-called mutual friend, and use a name that you can remember in case we need a follow-up on something here in the office.*

§

Thirty minutes later, the two of them had just finished ordering their lunches. Both of them were satisfied that the noise and clatter from the other patrons and the kitchen, which was next to their table, would completely cover their conversation.

Charlie was there representing the Sheriff's Department, which had been asked to step in and work with the U.S. Customs Department in Southern California. Charlie knew that he would enjoy listening to Ellen Burchett as she began the conversation with one of her great smiles.

Before she started the conversation, she took out of the large artistic-looking bag that she was carrying a large, white sealed envelope that had his name on it. Reading upside-down, Charlie could see that the lettering on the front of the envelope read: FOR THE EYES ONLY OF SHERIFF'S REPRESENTATIVE DETECTIVE CHARLIE GLASS.

Charlie knew that the envelope was to be taken with him and would not be opened up at this meeting. He was just there to listen and learn from the pretty lady who kept smiling at him from across the table.

Again from the super-large artistic-looking handbag she pulled out three black-and-white photographs of a man she identified as José Creto, a Mexican National. The photos were of José: a frontal head-shot, a side head shot and one from a distance to show his body shape and size.

Ellen was speaking softly, and Charlie had to lean across the small table in order to hear what she was saying. "His name is José Creto, and we believe that it is his job to set up the distribution system for the drugs that the Mexican Cartel would be sending into California. José and his thirteen companions were all video-recorded when they illegally landed on one of the beaches off the pier at Santa Monica beach. They were seen bringing in twelve large sealed boxes of narcotics from Mexico, along with some heavy-duty weapons.

"They were being watched and recorded by my own branch of the U.S. Customs group that I work for out of Los Angeles. We did not arrest or detain them in any way. All we wanted to do was to follow them and learn where their "safe house" was, so that we could get at them any time we wanted.

"The real danger here is that they were heavily armed with heavy-duty submachine guns, sniper rifles and high-powered handguns. If things come down to a shooting contest between our boys and these guys, who knows what will happen? We had to allow them to leave their landing site unmolested and undetected if we were going to learn anything about their plans in the future. So all we did was watch them load up their goods and take off in several trucks.

"And getting back to their leader José, who is known as a killer who will not hesitate to react with deadly force as he has reportedly done in the past, José is a very average-looking male who can fit into any crowd and any conversation either in English or Spanish. He is five foot nine and weights about one hundred and sixty pounds. Whenever José leaves the safe house, located on the west side of downtown L.A., he always has one of his. bodyguards with him, who came on that dark and windy night when they all hit the beach.

"The weapons and the drug merchandise that were going to be used as free samples for the contacts he would be making on the streets were all left behind under the careful eyes of the other Mexican nationals that he had brought over with him for backup if he needed any.

"I'll be closing down my office where we met today. I received word that I am being re-assigned—and in our business, that really means that somehow or other I made a mistake somewhere, and the Cartel is looking at me. That is why I asked you not to speak about anything of importance in my office. After lunch today, I'll be picked up by that black Caddy parked across the street and taken away to some other assignment outside of the West Coast where my life will not be in danger as I have been told that it now is."

They finished up their lunch talking about nothing in particular, and when finished, Charlie picked up the check and the envelope she had left for him.

Through the window in the front of the restaurant, Charlie watched Ellen get into the waiting car, which whisked her away. She gave him a smile and a wave to indicate that she knew the driver, and that everything was in order for her disappearance. Charlie would never see Ellen Burchett again and he thought that it was a sad thing because she was fun and interesting.

When Charlie returned to his office, he washed up, bought a candy bar from the machine in the hallway, and sat down and opened up the sealed envelope that Ellen had just given to him.

He knew that it would be interesting reading and that it would explain what the United States Customs Department wanted the Sheriff's Investigators to do to help them with their ongoing war against the drug trade. Charlie knew that he was about to read some fascinating stuff!

CHAPTER TWENTY-TWO

It read as follows:

TO CHARLIE GLASS – LEAD DETECTIVE FOR THE LOS ANGELES SHERIFF'S DEPARTMENT

FOR YOUR EYES ONLY

Hello, Detective Glass:

As follows please find an up-to-the-minute report on our investigation of the drug trade as it pertains to the immediate Southern California areas of San Diego and Los Angeles.

It is our understanding that drug enforcement has only been a minor problem for your area, up to recent events that will be impacting your area shortly.

It is our intent to give you within this short report a history and an up-to-date summary of who it was in the past that set the problem in motion, and who are the present suppliers, the present buyers and sellers of the product and our response to all of this.

§

The concept of money laundering regulations goes back to ancient times, and is intertwined with the development of money and banking.

Money laundering is first seen with individuals who were hiding their wealth from the state in order to avoid taxation or confiscation or a combination of both.

In China around the year two thousand BCE, merchants would hide their wealth from the rulers, who simply would take it away from them and then banish them from the country. In addition to hiding their valuables, they would move money around and invest it in businesses in remote provinces or even outside of China.

Over the millennia since then, many rulers and states imposed rules that would take wealth from their own citizens, and this led directly to offshore banking and tax evasion.

In the twentieth century, the seizing of wealth again became popular when it was seen as an additional crime-preventing tool. For the first time, during the period of Prohibition in the United States, taxes were being claimed by the government. This was in the 1930s. It was organized crime that received the biggest boost from Prohibition as a large source of new funds that they were able to get by the illegal sales of alcohol.

Historically, organized crime groups in the United States had tended to form around a shared ethnic identity. The organized crime groups, which were street gangs such as the Jewish, Irish and Italian gangs, all sprang up around the entire country in the nineteenth century. The gangs gave immigrant youths a measure of protection and a sense of belonging in a society that generally marginalized and discriminated against them. It is perhaps not surprising that as the early street gangs evolved into purely criminal organizations; they tended to maintain a strong ethnic orientation, shared background, customs and trust for each other.

The head of the Mafia operating out of the east coast was Meyer Lansky, who saw a huge opportunity to increase their profits by forging a tight relationship with the Cuban dictator Fulgencio Batista. Batista's willingness to work with the Lansky/ Mafia organization brought to Cuba a partnership of corruption that spread widely throughout the entire Cuban government as the Mafia turned out tremendous profits for everyone by running the gambling casinos.

But Cuba's mobster paradise would prove to be short-lived. Fidel Castro, who led the Communist overthrow of the Batista dictatorship in 1959, actively rid his country of any and all Mafia influences.

Meyer Lansky and the boys fled the country, taking millions of dollars of illegal Cuban gambling money with them. The Lansky operation now had the millions of dollars it always wanted and needed to move their criminal activities into high gear.

While Lansky had finished draining the Cuban economy for the Mafia, the anti-communist United States government tried to get rid of Fidel Castro but failed miserably in their efforts. The most famous memory that everyone has of this time is the famous Bay of Pigs collapse of forces backed by the United States government attacking Cuba. This tremendous failure was compounded when the United States government (CIA) cut loose all the Cuban nationals it had trained. Most of them drifted into the United States, and there was now a major presence of scores of men who were highly trained in the use of automatic weapons and explosives.

One of the first of the CIA-trained Cubans to make a mark in American organized crime was a former vice cop with strong ties to Meyer Lansky himself. José Miguel Battle used the shady alliances he had forged in Cuba to gain a foothold in illegal gambling in both Florida and California. He was very careful to give Meyer Lansky's Mafia a piece of the action, and he never really had any problem from "the boys back east".

As we know, this arrangement was able to continue until the 1980s when finally the Mafia had to stage a withdrawal from the west coast after their leading partner in the area, Leonardo da Vinci, was killed by the Los Angeles Sheriff's Department in a gun battle. When the Mafia pulled themselves completely out of the west coast, opportunities opened up for newcomers like the previously mentioned José Battle, formerly from the Cuban islands.

Battle began sending CIA-trained enforcers to expand the territory of his gambling and numbers operations. These enforcers barged in on independent street gangs who were running hundreds of small storefront gambling operations. Under threat from the enforcers, the locals had to turn over the "lion's share" of their profits. Locals who balked at this demand for their money generally paid with their lives if they refused. They just could not compete with this new organization that was now freely roaming the streets.

Battle's reputation in Los Angeles was one of terror. He had a reputation locally of freely blowing up cars and burning down stores of anyone who defied him.

This loosely brings us up to where we are in today's world, and I close my report with a request for a meeting between your local Sheriff's Department and some of our government representatives. Please respond to this letter ASAP so we can meet and set up a plan of action that will work for all of us.

My very best regards,
Michael Mistaf

CHAPTER TWENTY-THREE

Charlie put the letter down on the green blotter that covered about half of his desktop. He just sat there quietly as he reviewed in his mind the letter he had just read.

Most everything that Michael Mistaf had brought up in it was not new to him. He knew about the Mafia in Southern California because he was very involved in getting them to leave. He knew about how drugs and illegal funding was finding their way onto the streets of Los Angeles, and how the various gangs and drug lords were killing each other over territory rights.

The policy that came down to him from the Sheriff himself was to stand back and observe only as the dealers and their backers killed each other. Both the Sheriff's Department and the LAPD were united in playing the waiting game. The more the drugs dealers killed off each other meant fewer people on the street pushing their products.

The additional thing that the letter was alerting him to, besides the locals going after each other, which was old news, was informing him that the Mexicans were wanting to get into the game. It was the millions of dollars that passed from hand to hand in the area that had caught their eye.

Charlie was comfortable with them eliminating each other, but from what the United States Customs and Drug Enforcement agency was telling him, there would shortly be two new players who wanted to get their slice of the pie. Besides the local gangs, the Bloods and the Crips, there would now be two new organizations, both of them from Mexico.

The person called José Creto and his thirteen men, weapons and products for sale that had recently landed on the beach were only the tip of the iceberg. They were the first of two groups. They were probably here to test the potential for their products and then, after setting up some sort of distribution system, would return to Mexico to report back to the big boys.

And the thought of setting up the network by these guys got Charlie to thinking that this might be the chance he was waiting for to bring his department's mole out of the darkness and into the light of discovery. He tabled this idea for the moment and thought about the rest of the letter he had just read.

Narcotics agent Michael Mistaf also mentioned a name that he had been hearing lately. It appeared that the second player in this new game was going to be José Creto, another Mexican National who had survived the Cuban disaster and brought over a bunch of enforcers who were trained by the CIA in weapons and violence.

Charlie knew that if he played the card he had just been dealt by the Narcotics agent, he might have another job for Danny Ossen, who was still the only detective in his department that he could really trust. He thought that Danny would jump into Charlie's plan with both feet. After all, he really owned Charlie a big return favor for the Rita Rose sting that led to her arrest.

Danny was still talking about his role in the sting with Rita, and he was always saying that if she wasn't a hooker, he would be after her as someone to date and have a lot of laughs with. Not only did Danny say that she was fun and that she loved to laugh a lot, but that she was also a real looker and absolutely great in bed. Danny said that in his mind, she was the perfect woman with only one fault, and this saddened him when he said what her fault was. She was the damned madam to the stars. That killed any possible relationship that he might have had with her if he had met her as just a regular beautiful girl wandering around Hollywood.

Charlie was positive that Danny Ossen would jump all over the opportunity to work with Charlie again, especially on the attempt to catch the elusive "rat" in Charlie's department.

Charlie put the letter back in the envelope, got up from his desk and deposited it into the private wall safe provided to him, and left for the day. He was going to take Sweetpea out to dinner and talk about his ideas as they enjoyed a good meal at one of the local restaurants.

CHAPTER TWENTY-FOUR

In Los Angeles there are many famous delis. One of the favorites for both Sweetpea and Charlie was called Canter's Deli and it had been open for business seemingly forever. It was located not too far from their offices in downtown Los Angeles, a few blocks away from the famous landmark area called the Fairfax district, home to the world-famous Farmers Market, where Sweetpea often would do her shopping for fresh fruits and vegetables.

Canter's Deli was where they had decided to eat their dinner, and the casual surroundings, the noise and the wonderful smells were just what they both needed to relax and enjoy each other's company as they always did.

While they were waiting for their food to come, Sweetpea told Charlie that she wanted to share a funny story with him that was making the rounds at her office in the Sheriff's record department where she has been working.

"A man walks into a private bank and says to the lady employee behind the counter, 'I want to open up a fucking bank account.'

The lady employee is shocked and quickly runs to the manager, tells him the story, and brings him back with her to the waiting customer. The manager looks the man up and down and then says to him, 'What seems to be the problem here?'

The man replies, 'I have this suitcase with one hundred thousand dollars in it, and I want to open a fucking bank account.'

The bank manager looks at the man and his suitcase, hesitates for a moment or two and then replies, 'What? And this bitch won't help you?'"

Sweetpea laughed and laughed at her own joke as Charlie just sat there quietly looking at her. Fortunately, their dinner arrived and they did not have to continue the conversation over Sweetpea's joke as they began to eat.

Over the ice-cream sundaes that they had for dessert, Charlie thought that he needed to add something to the conversation, so he went into a topic he was well acquainted with, and one that he knew Sweetpea would understand. "Great story about the bank, Sweetpea! Let me try out one of mine on you.

"Think about a typical day in your own life. You get up in the morning and you get dressed. You put on a new skirt that you just bought and a button pops off it as you put it on. You paid $150 for the skirt because it was made in Italy by a famous designer. You paid more for it because of the name on the label! But what you didn't know was that the skirt was not manufactured in Italy, but in southeast Asia at a factory controlled by an Asian organized-crime group that manufactures knock-offs of everything from Rolex watches to Louis Vuitton luggage.

"You get into your car and you drive to work. Traffic is terrible. A car has broken down and is blocking traffic. The engine stalled because there is dirt in the gas line. The car's owner bought gas at a small gas station that purchased its product from a company that is controlled by organized crime guys who buy low and thin out the gasoline with things that later on will cause engine problems.

"A little later on, your traffic slows again! Construction on the highway is resurfacing the roadway. The contractor who was originally awarded the paving contract had Mob connections and was able to rig the bid. But to make money at that reduced price, they only put down a half inch of asphalt instead of the bid-upon full inch. When the city inspector came to check the quality of the work, he was given five hundred dollars in cash to "look the other way" and approve the project.

"And finally, another story that has stayed with me all these years.

"Some years ago, a local bank had called the police because they thought they had spotted a pair of money launderers. An older Italian guy had come into the branch with a younger, well-dressed bodyguard type of guy with him. As they waited in line for their turn with the teller, the bodyguard kept going to the front window of the bank and looking up and down the street. It was obvious that the man was checking for any visible police activity.

"At the teller's window, the older Italian man removed close to a half a million dollars in cash from a bag that he was carrying and tells the teller that he wants to open an account and make a cash deposit. The money that he began laying out was old, and mostly full of dirt. The teller was convinced that it was loot from some old bank robbery or kidnapping, and she pressed the emergency button under her window, which alerted the bank manager to call the police.

"What was really happening was that the old guy was the grandfather, and the "bodyguard" was, in reality, his grandson. The grandson was visiting his grandfather and discovered that the old man had been hiding money all over his house and had even been burying it in his backyard for years. The young man became alarmed, and with good reason. The formerly traditional Italian immigrant neighborhood where the grandfather lived had over the years been taken over by crackheads and prostitutes, and was very dangerous for an old man who lived alone. So the grandson finally convinced the old boy, who did not trust banks, that he had to secure his money, and that was why the two of them appeared at the bank, where they were now talking to the police.

"But what about the bodyguard acting so nervous and keeping an eye on the street? Well, it turned out that he had parked his car in a no-stopping zone and was afraid of being towed away.

"The final point of this story is that when people are trying to pick out the bad guys, they are usually looking for the Don Corleone from *The Godfather,* when maybe they should be looking for Don Knotts. And that, Sweetpea, my love, is the entire point. Criminals look just like you and me. They are not going to look like the bad guys you see in the movies."

Charlie paid the bill, escorted the beautiful lady that he loved out of the restaurant, and they were soon in the car on their way back to her apartment for an evening of wild and passionate lovemaking. For Charlie, it was the perfect ending to a perfect evening.

CHAPTER TWENTY-FIVE

An important and highly secret meeting was being set up in Central Los Angeles at the newly remodeled Lancaster Hotel on Main and Figueroa Street just opposite the headquarters for the Los Angeles Public Library. The place was selected because of the amazing number of people who were always moving about outside this central location. There were always new faces circulating in case anyone was watching the area.

The Lancaster Hotel, unknown to almost everyone, was owned and operated by the leftover Mafia members, who still had their fingers in a lot of little things that were always going down in this central area. On the second floor of the hotel there was a specially constructed large conference room that was used by the general public for important meetings, and by the Mob when they needed the specific services of what the meeting room offered.

In addition to the wonderful food and drinks that were always provided for them from the restaurants downstairs, they also had use of the completely hidden video and audio cameras that would record everything that went on. One wall had a beautiful floor-to-ceiling mirror that reflected everyone and everything back into the room. Not only was this mirror able to reflect back whatever was going on inside the room, but it had a special two-way mirror that would allow someone in the small room on the other side of the mirror to see into the big room and not be seen by anyone on the other side looking into the mirror.

It was this specially mirrored room that was being used for this meeting, that was just being called to order by the hotel manager, Ernesto. He was the only one of over twenty people within the room who knew who the person was that could not be seen through the mirror, and yet could be easily heard over the loudspeaker which was specially made to change his voice and making it unrecognizable.

The room was set up with Ernesto standing at the central table and looking around at the silent people who were staring at him. Ernesto introduced himself as the number-two man in the chain of command whose responsibility it was to see that the various operations being run by this new organization were going smoothly. He explained that they could supply unlimited narcotics from Mexico, unlimited heavy-duty weapons like submachine guns and sniper rifles that were available upon short notice, etc.

He also explained that in exchange for a ten-percent rake-off from the profits that were out there on the streets for the taking, they would get complete advance information on any raids, movements or interference directed at them from law enforcement, which was made up of three individual agencies combining their efforts in their war against drugs and street violence. Everyone knew that he was talking about the Los Angeles Police Department, the Sheriff's Department and the local offices of the Federal Bureau of Investigation, who were working together in a huge program to crack down on drug traffic and the violence it caused in the streets of Southern California.

Ernesto thanked them for their attention and asked them to listen to his immediate superior who had a few words for them. He explained that they had all been watched through the one-way looking glass that they could see dominating the entire wall behind them.

A clear and pleasant voice came at them from out of the loud speakers that were placed around the room. It was obvious that the voice was electronically altered so that the voice they were hearing could not be recognized.

"Thank you all for being here. I shall keep my comments short and right to the point.

"Since you are all sitting here, right now, at this moment in time, it is obvious that you are known to me and to the people who stand behind me. When you are talking with Ernesto, who is well known among you all, you will be speaking to me through him. Ernesto is empowered to provide you with all of your needs, wants and desires as you go out into our community to sell your products.

"We do not sell anything; you all do that. We do not provide the muscle needed to defend your rights and territories; you do that. We do nothing to guide you or tell you what to do. You are here because we have investigated each and every one of you and found you worthy of joining our brotherhood.

"If you know of anyone in your position who is out there on the streets and who is not in this room, kindly look for them in the next 100 days to see if they are still around. I am suggesting that you will find them to be absent from the local scene, and causing their disappearance is what we do. We will slowly but surely eliminate your competition out there on the streets, thereby increasing your profits and domination of your individual territory. In return, our 10% cut off the top will be pennies on the dollars that you will be adding to your net worth.

"To oppose us in this is to die. It is that simple, because there is nowhere you can run and hide from us. We know who you are, where you are, and how to get at you. If we destroy you, the organization that you have worked so hard to build up will go to someone else who is sitting somewhere in this room, right now, looking at the glass mirror behind which I am comfortably sitting, enjoying the great food. Your choice is simple. Join us or die. No exceptions, no deviations.

"In closing, I wish to advise you that all arrangements for your continued good fortune will be handled through our common associate Ernesto. When talking about me, understand that the one and only thing that I am giving to you in return for our 10% of your income is protection from law enforcement. Kindly refer to me in all further conversations as "the man.""

"Thank you for your attention. Ernesto will fill you in on all the details. Whatever your needs are for men, material, weapons and so on will be handled through him.

"Remember we offer you immunity from the law, personal protection, and a fortune in illegally gotten gains though your own efforts. I bid you good day.""

CHAPTER TWENTY-SIX

It was official. Danny Ossen had been taken off of his busywork desk and promoted to Charlie Glass's Detective Division as his number two. This meant that Danny would be allowed to go into any and all of the Sheriff's files, and that he could command any one of the Sheriff's Deputies at any time.

Charlie, who knew that Danny would shortly be promoted upon his own personal request, had kept Danny in the working loop and had all reports and paperwork forwarded to him while he was waiting for the promotion to come down. Charlie did this so that Danny would be immediately up and running when he stepped into the position as number two.

Therefore, when all the paperwork was finally in order, Danny moved into his new office, which was next to Charlie's and connected to it by a common door. Charlie has requested this first meeting for the two of them to meet in Danny's office. They each had a steaming cup of coffee in front of them. Each had a small identical set of papers that they had had the opportunity to look through before this meeting. This was to be a planning session, and Danny was to take the lead on all of the items except for the last and most important one.

Charlie had all calls held so that there would be no ringing telephones to bother them, and they were able to breeze through the majority of the items in a short period of time. Both of them were eager to get at the last item on the agenda, which was a report dealing with the sudden decrease in street violence.

A decrease in street violence was like a red flag that indicated that something different was happening. Obviously, it had to be determined what was causing this to happen. They both knew that as soon as things turned away from the normal way of doing things, something new had to have been added to the mix.

The report told them that there had been an increase in violent deaths. Seven street gang leaders were murdered, and then there was complete silence on all fronts. It was as if the city was a crime-free zone for about sixty days, and then everything went back to normal except for the beatings and shootings, which practically disappeared. This was not a normal pattern.

Danny Ossen knew Charlie well enough to know when it was time for him to stop talking. The look on Charlie's face was the same look that he had when he was working out the plot that they used to catch Rita Rose. Charlie was an excellent planner. Obviously, Charlie was going to suggest some sort of plan that would involve them both and Danny was all ears.

Charlie's thoughts, plans and schemes were usually very successful, and if he was reading Charlie right, he was about to make some sort of presentation for Danny to consider. And the interesting thing about one-on-one meetings that these two co-workers and friends had had in the past was that they usually came away with a scheme of some sort.

Danny sat quietly as Charlie got up from his chair and began to pace the small office.

"Danny, what I am going to say is for you to hear only and not to be repeated to anyone without my specific authorization. I don't want to get excited, but I think I see a light at the end of the tunnel regarding the "mole" in our midst that I have been talking about. I really think that I have come up with something, and I think that you and I should leave the office shortly and go out to dinner to talk about it.

"Even though I am sure that our offices are not bugged, I am not comfortable talking about the mole here where it is possible that someone could be listening to us. I have some papers to sign that will take me about an hour to look over. Meet me downstairs at the back entrance to the parking lot in an hour and let's walk over to the Pantry Restaurant on 9th and Figueroa. It is a noisy place, lots of fun things going on like singing servers, and it is owned by one of our former mayors. It will be a perfect place to talk."

Almost one hour from their last conversation, the two friends and co-workers were seated in the restaurant waiting for one of the waiters to walk over and take their order.

Charlie opened up the dialogue. "Danny, I could be way off base, but over the years I have told you that the mole or rat in our department has to be one of two guys that are high up in the Sheriff's Department. Without going into all the reasons that I have to suspect that one of these two guy is the villain in this life drama, let me tell you what only came to light within the last thirty day or so that has allowed me to point my finger at one of the two suspects that I have been watching carefully for a long time.

"Either one of the two could have been my number-two guy like you are now, but I could not trust either of them as long as things did not clean themselves up as they suddenly have done right now. I made you my number two because I can trust you, and we do work well together. So here is my promise and commitment you. You are my trusted number two, and you will stay that way with me as long as you want to be.

"Either Joe Wahl or Roberto Sanchez would have been named as my number two, but I have been uncomfortable with the two of them. There always was no doubt in my mind that one of them was the middleman for the crime families, but I could not prove things one way or another. Things have changed in the past few months, and I do believe that I know who is the mole, and I want to pass my thoughts by you so that we can come up with a plan of action.

"But first you have to read this confidential and final report regarding the capture and killing of the Mafia's leader here in L.A. His name was Leonardo Da Vinci XVIII, and he always claimed the original Leonardo as his relative. Anyway, we had Da Vinci cornered out on the pier at Santa Monica, and it was the outcome of this capture-and-kill that led me to believe that out of all the possible suspects who could be connected to the crime and violence in the city, only our two guys, Joe Wahl and Roberto Sanchez, jumped out at me as the only possible insiders from our department who could be the mole.

"Here are a few pages of the final report that will show you why I am sure our guy is one of these two insiders."

Without another word being spoken, Charlie sipped quietly at his coffee, and Danny Ossen started to read the evidence report that he was given.

§

FINAL COPY AND REPORT ON THE DEATH OF LEONARDO DA VINCI—LEADER OF LOCAL MAFIA ORGANIZATION WITHIN THE CITY OF LOS ANGELES, CALIFORNIA

Fugitive described as Leonardo da Vinci XVIII sighted with at least ten companions at the Santa Monica Pier, located in Santa Monica, Calif.

Full response requested as the sighting has been verified by police spotter via helicopter.

All responding officers are to be in full riot/protective gear.

Los Angeles Sheriff's Department to take lead with the Los

Angeles Police Department to act as backup.

Chain of command:

- Sheriff's Detective Charlie Glass as primary.
- Sheriff's Detective Joe Wahl as second.
- Sheriff's Department SWAT Chief Roberto Sanchez as overall field commander.

Bomb squad and SWAT teams are required to be in full protective gear at all times due to explosive software noted in front of office at end of pier.

§

The area noted as the Santa Monica Pier was listed in the Sheriff's location book as being officially called Pacific Ocean Park. The amusement park is located at the end of the large, free-standing Santa Monica Pier, which projects directly out onto the Pacific Ocean in the direction of nearby Catalina Island. It is the only amusement park on the west coast of the United States that is completely located on a free-standing pier.

There are a total of thirteen rides within the park, including the world's only solar-powered Ferris wheel. The park provides an unrestricted view of the Pacific Ocean from anywhere within the park, and it has one world-famous roller-coaster that completely encircles the entire park.

CHAPTER TWENTY-SEVEN

Danny finished the reading of the file just as the waiter came over to their table to take their order. Since the meal was going to be taken care of by the Sheriff's Department budget, both men ordered what would usually be called a "hearty" breakfast.

It was Danny who reopened the conversation. "I am familiar with the contents of the report, but I never had the opportunity to read the official version. According to what it said, the only thing you really accomplished was the elimination of da Vinci and the mob from the scene. It did not say anything concrete about the "rat in the pack," and I assume something new has come up, since we are sitting here talking about it".

Charlie replied, "I am sure you will understand what I mean when I say that my nose has picked up the scent of the bad guy, and the smell is strong enough for me to react to it. Beyond a shadow of a doubt in my mind, I can name the mole right now, but proving it is another thing—and that is what we are here to discuss right now." Charlie watched as Danny turned over a paper napkin from the table, covered up what he was writing with his other hand, wrote a few words and handed it to Charlie face-down.

Danny continued, "Unless I am mistaken, and I rarely am in a situation like this, the name I wrote on the other side of that napkin is the name you are about to tell me. For all the weeks that I was sitting downstairs in the busy room doing nothing but filling up space, waiting for my new number-two job to get approved, I dug into your problem with the mole and came to what I hope was the right guy who was playing his underground games with you. and who you are now going to call the "mole." He gestured at Charlie to turn over the napkin and watched as he did so.

A big smile lit up Charlie Glass's face as he read the writing on the napkin.

Based upon my personal research and the reading of the many hints that you let drop, I believe our mole is Detective Joe Wahl.

The smile on Charlie's face was enough for Danny to know that he was right-on with his assumption, and both men seemed pleased with each other.

Charlie ripped up the napkin that had the writing on it and started working on the breakfast that had just arrived. Danny did the same and the conversation time changed to eating time as both detectives dug into the meal that was set before them.

§

As they walked slowly back to their offices, Charlie was pretty much dominating the conversation. It was just that he had so much to say, and Danny needed to hear everything that was on Charlie's mind in order to get himself brought up to speed.

Charlie began, "Let's talk about Roberto Sanchez for a moment and clear up a few things so that we can forget about him in connection with the mole. I had assigned Roberto as our contact with the FBI in order to get him away from the daily goings-on at the office. I have been getting nothing but compliments on him coming from their headquarters.

"On the date in question when 'the big meeting' was being held downtown, Roberto was out of town on assignment. This definitely clears him of having anything to do with being the bad guy. He just was not there when they were conducting their business. With Roberto notably absent, we have a clean and clear tape recording made of what was going on at that meeting.

"We were able to wire up one of their guys whom we had caught red-handed in a robbery, and rather than face heavy jail time, he agreed to be an informer for us on anything that came his way that would be of interest to us. Based on the evidence from the wire that our guy was carrying at that meeting, we know that the dozens of gang killings that recently happened were their internal housecleaning. They were cleaning up loose ends.

"After those killings that quickly followed the meeting, the streets of Los Angeles became pure again, and for weeks on end nothing, absolutely nothing was happening. We now know why, and that mystery is solved. The gangs were reorganizing themselves according to the dictates of the new leader who seems to have emerged in their midst.

"This new guy, who asked everyone to call him 'the man,' named Ernesto Villa as his number two, and all problems and suggestions were to come and go through him. Ernesto Villa is well known to us even though he has never been found guilty of anything that would stick to him.

"Two days after the big meeting, our inside wired guy dropped off his equipment and told us that we were now squared away. If he was ever caught wearing anything other than his regular clothes, then he would be a dead man. I was told that he quickly left the Los Angeles area and headed for the action that was going on in Miami Beach. This was probably the smartest move he had ever made in his life.

"As a result of this major meeting of so many of the local bad guys now under the rule of their hidden leader who calls himself 'the man,' we now know that the local street gangs have all been brought together with the imported Mexicans and their illegal guns and their narcotics. Normally we would say that this is a bad thing, but I don't really think so.

"We now know who the leader is, and we know that he slipped up by calling the big meeting when Roberto was out of town. It allowed us to put the finger on him because there was no way that he could have known that Roberto had an assignment to carry out elsewhere, and that his leaving was a last-minute thing. This accident in timing is just what we have been waiting for, and all that we have to do is to make it work in our favor.

"What is most interesting is that 'the man,' or Joe Wahl, as we call him, is right here under our noses working at our place. And if we get 'the man,' we get his organization that is running around in our streets. Maybe we can get a two-for-one outcome out of all this?"

A smiling Charlie Glass and a happy Danny Ossen ended their pleasant walk, entered into the Sheriff's station and went their separate ways.

CHAPTER TWENTY-EIGHT

It was now several weeks later and the busy streets of Los Angeles were back to hosting the usual crime events that have always been happening in the greater L.A. neighborhoods.

The threat of violence, rather than violence itself, was enough to keep things moving along at the proper level of profits for the new organization working for "the man." Ernesto, who was the number-two man for the organization, had personally hired José Creto, who came into Santa Monica Bay one dark and stormy night along with thirteen men to provide the muscle for when they finally got around to selling the huge number of Mexican drugs that they now had on hand.

All of these things were known to Charlie at the Sheriff's Central Operations Center, where his well-paid-for information would come to him from the street and from several other very highly paid informants within the newly formed organization.

Charlie was thinking that Joe Wahl missed his calling for not being a professional actor. Joe was doing everything he was supposed to be doing for his day job with the Sheriff's Department, and at night he led his secret double life as the top of the new and highly successful criminal organization that he had put together with Ernesto.

Ernesto was an interesting find for Joe. Behind his great smile and well-dressed looks, Ernesto was a pure killer who had no mercy in his dealings on the street. He had come to Los Angeles by way of Miami Beach, where things got a bit hot for him with several warrants out for his arrest upon murder charges.

The Miami Beach police department had sent an urgent memo to the Los Angeles Sheriff's Detective division that he was on his way by train. The message was picked up by Joe Wahl, and telling no one where he was going, he met the train at the downtown station and flashed his badge at Ernesto, and then took him out to lunch, where they got acquainted with each other. The bonding between the two like-minded criminals was there right from the start.

Joe had Ernesto move into a personal safe house that he ran for his special street friends, and after a week or two for Ernesto to settle in and get the feel for the streets of L.A., they sat down and made plans.

Ernesto, of course, was originally from Mexico, where he had several strong contacts among the controlling drug cartel members. It was Ernesto who went into Mexico and met with some of his old drug-dealing friends and worked out the plan with them as discussed with his new associate Joe Wahl.

The deal was simplicity itself. Joe Wahl would provide the necessary protection on the streets of Southern California, put up the necessary funds to get things going, while at the same time, by using some of his personal batch of enforcers, eliminate the heads of the local street gangs who had been around for many years and had grown careless in their safety habits.

It was Ernesto who had sent for José Creto and his crew of thirteen killers to hit the beach on that dark and stormy night. It was Joe Wahl who funded all expenses and set up the internal working of the new criminal group that he was now beginning to deploy. The combination of Ernesto and Joe Wahl worked well, and it was just a matter of months until they had their now-famous dinner meeting that set all things in motion.

It was only a few weeks later that Charlie Glass was giving final instructions to two undercover agents that he had borrowed from the FBI. He was carefully looking over the two detectives who would be going out in the field to straighten out a few things that needed to be worked on.

He had brought in Beth Ruthman, an out-of-town detective, to play the part of the female diversion, and another out-of-towner to play the male lead. His name was Blake Goodman, and he looked the part of an ever-so-smooth con-man.

Beth looked great, wearing baggy black high-waisted pants and a cotton T-shirt that fit her like a tight-fitting second skin. Her face was tan and flawless, and her makeup was so subtle that it was like she was wearing none at all.

Blake's suit was gray with a slight sheen to it, and his shirt was white and crisp and immaculate.

Together they were perfect for the image that Charlie wanted to project of a well-dressed, well connected to the world of crime, quite professional and very much into-the-moment couple.

CHAPTER TWENTY-NINE

In Los Angeles, the Santee Alley is one of the most popular retail/ wholesale shopping areas in the entire Los Angeles Fashion District of the downtown area. It is best known for its festival-like atmosphere and amazing bargains.

Santee Alley's one hundred and fifty-plus stores and vendors sell everything for the entire family such as accessories, toys, perfume, gift items and usually a great deal of drugs being sold from behind the innocent-looking store fronts.

Santee Alley is really an actual alley, located between Santee Street and Maple Ave and from Olympic Boulevard to 12th Street.

It is open three hundred and sixty-five days a year including holidays. All businesses in the Alley are privately owned and operated by local merchants. Most locations open at nine-thirty in the morning and close about nine o'clock at night.

§

Charlie Glass and his number-two guy Danny Ossen were once again sitting and talking softly over their coffee in one of the nearby coffee shops where they were sure that their conversation would not have other listeners. They were within easy walking distance of their offices in case they were paged to come in for something that needed their attention.

Charlie could not have one of the Sheriff's specialists sweep their offices for outside listening devices because if he did so that would definitely be a signal to Joe Wahl that something was going on around him. This was something that Charlie did not want to happen, and so they once again were meeting in the coffee shop.

Charlie was saying, "Forging an identity is like aging a good bottle of fine wine! You can't rush it, and you have to follow certain steps. We will be opening up checking, savings and credit-card accounts at several local banks under the assumed names of our newly assigned special government agents. The FBI is handling the money problem, and hundreds of thousands of dollars will shortly show in their accounts if anyone decides to look at them.

"I thought that this would be a good idea because I am sure that Ernesto or Joe would be investigating the funding available for Blake Goodman and Beth Ruthman. Our case against Joe Wahl will live or die with the quality of these two undercover agents, and they are both said to be the best at what they do.

"We also have working for us some 'reliable turncoats' whom our Sheriff's Department caught red-handed with their fingers in the cookie jar. They were facing some heavy-duty jail time, and in return for their making the introductions for our two undercover agents, they agreed to leave the Southern California area, never to return. These informers have given us lists of names and business for Blake and Beth to seek out as they work the Santee Alley district.

"These Mexican informers, who are now our valuable assets, were not what is known among the Italian gangsters as "made men." To be a "made man", they would have to be of Italian descent, and have carried out a contract killing or a specific job for an Italian Mob family.

"These guys whom we turned around to work with us had all worked with different local crime groups. They were dealing drugs, running guns, committing extortion plots and doing simple bodyguard work. Every one of these guys who are now working with us seem friendly enough. But beneath the surface we know them to be very calculating and lethal killers. People around them often developed the bad habit of turning up with multiple gunshot wounds to the back of their heads. A fringe benefit after the Joe Wahl affair finally ends is that we will be rid of these informants of ours, as they will head back to Miami Beach, where most of them originally came from.

"To get the specific evidence we need to make this case stick against Joe Wahl and Ernesto, we needed high-quality, reliable recording equipment that could easily be hidden in a briefcase or handbag. The wiring of a small microphone will be hidden inside the lining of both handbag and suitcase and our department will be able to run back the sound tapes through a playback system that will bring up any muffled or distant voices to perfect clarity. We will be installing two separate microphones in each of our agents' handbags or suitcases in case the person or persons that they will be dealing with were on the other side of the handbag or suitcase.

"And here is the interesting part of how cash from these narcotics sales were converted by Joe Wahl into clean dollars. Ernesto would drive around town, with plenty of bodyguards with him, and convert the cash received from the sale of drugs on the street into cashier's checks from the local banks. He would always keep his purchased cashier's checks below the $10,000 maximum that would automatically trigger a report to the United States government.

"Ernesto's family, friends or business associates in the Los Angeles area would then deposit these cashier's checks into their personal and proper accounts. From this now clean and washed money, Ernesto would take out of the banks cashier's checks in the amounts of $50,000 for the purchase of more narcotics from across the border. There he would trade these clean and proper cashier's checks to the Mexican cartel's business man, who would act as a middleman for more drugs to be smuggled into Ernesto's safe houses, which would then be put out on the streets of Los Angeles.

"This is a tricky operation, but things are going well for Joe Wahl and friends, and the new organization is making millions of dollars for them all. And with Ernesto as the front man, things had seemed to be going well for the organization until the slip-up occurred with Roberto Sanchez being out of town at the wrong moment.

"The wrong moment for them was when the meeting that they originally held with Joe Wahl talking to everyone from behind the two-way mirror happened while the other suspect Roberto Sanchez was away on FBI business and could not be connected with the goings-on."

Only Joe Wahl could be connected to all of this, and out of the two suspects that Charlie could never separate from each other, events now did it for him, with Roberto gone, and Joe tied in by the informers who were at the meeting. Charlie was now ready to use the special services of Beth Ruthman and Blake Goodman to bring everything to light and allow them to make a strong case against Joe Wahl.

Charlie advised his two new agents that they could spend any amount of money that was required for the stylish clothing that they would need to carry off their entrapment as they worked their way up the ladder to meet with Ernesto and Joe Wahl.

The look that they needed to achieve was most important because experienced criminals like Ernesto and his associates would be looking at these two new wannabes very carefully. Every feature would be examined before they became accepted into the culture of the underworld drug enterprises. A flaw in the smallest detail could send any possible growing relationship into the trashcan. These details absolutely included the clothes that they were wearing.

In addition to wearing designer clothing, special attention had to be paid to their shoes. The agents would probably be sitting across the room from the dealers, and when our "guys" would cross their legs, the bad guys would be looking directly at their shoes. They could not have holes in the soles of their shoes, or be wearing shoes or nylons that could be purchased at any Sears-Roebuck store. They were also aware that our agents would have their hotel rooms searched and their clothing in the closets had to play perfectly into the part of wealthy buyers just looking to make contacts.

The FBI had trained their body language to fit into the pattern of who they said they were. The bad guys would be looking for certain mannerisms that some cops can't seem to get rid of.

It was also stressed that they not use police talk. Certain words like "violators," "ten-four," and policing words like that were dead give aways.

They were also taught to use little Italian phrases and to throw them into their conversations. Italians are always well thought of.

CHAPTER THIRTY

It was a beautiful day in Los Angeles and the temperature was somewhere in the low seventies with a touch of a spring breeze in the air. Beth Ruthman and Blake Goodman were carrying a few shopping bags full of small purchases that they had made as they walked slowly down the central downtown Los Angeles' Santee Alley pathway that was leading them toward the back end of the huge open shopping area. To all outward appearances, they seemed to be just another young couple enjoying the shops and the wonderful weather as they moved from open shop to open shop.

The reality was that they were the advance undercover Sheriff's team being sent into the area to follow up on Lead Detective Charlie Glass's belief that his informants were telling him the truth when they told him that the new leader in volume sales of drugs imported from Mexico, were being sold in large-quantity orders out of booth sixty-nine at the Santee Alley shopping area.

The handsome couple was dressed quite casually and yet gave off the impression of wealth and power as they walked along with the sun glittering off of the bracelets and jewelry each of them were wearing. Slowly they were working their way toward the end of the open-ended shops, and stopped at the very next to the last display booth located just under the sign which posted this store number as sixty-eight. While they were looking over some of the

137

merchandise next door to their targeted area, their attention was directed at the next booth, number sixty-nine.

There were no customers that they could see. The only visible person appeared to be the young Hispanic salesgirl who was folding up some of the towels that were being displayed for sale.

Blake was the first one to walk over with a big smile on his handsome face for the young salesgirl, who replied to his greeting in Spanish of *"Buenas días."* He picked up a few items and set most of them down as he gave off the appearance of looking for something to buy.

Following up Blake's entry into the small, open booth, Beth engaged the store girl in a conversation over one of the items that they had on sale. She had the complete attention of the girl, which allowed Blake to slip into the closed but unlocked back room where he was able to quickly look around.

What he saw in that quick look encouraged him greatly. He was looking at a spotless, huge black desk that had a large monitor screen connected to what looked like a simple and basic computer. It was early in the use of computers, and seeing this model told Blake that the storefront with the salesgirl out there was only a cover-up for other things that seemed to be going on inside. He only had a moment before he had to exit the room and his eyes quickly picked out a letter written out in Spanish with today's date on it and a letterhead which read "the man."

Blake touched nothing and quickly backed out of the room and stepped down the single step that put him amid the store's merchandise. He briskly walked toward the front of the open booth and said a few things to the young girl, and taking the newly purchased shopping bag with some towels in it from his companion, he quietly escorted Beth out of the area and back toward the front street leading to their car, which was parked at one of the lots on Santee Street.

There was great excitement in their car as they hurried back to see Charlie Glass and confirm his hunch that booth sixty-nine at the Santee Street Outlets was indeed somehow connected to the heavy-duty drug operations that were going on within the city limits.

A happy Charlie Glass bundled his latest Sheriff's Department insider group off to one of the finest local restaurants for an evening of fine food, a few drinks, and lots of conversation concerning how they were going to deal with the organization being run by "the man."

It was a Wednesday night and the Pacific Dining Car Restaurant was not crowded at all, and Charlie was able to get immediate seating for his party of five.

That party of five sitting at the huge round dinner table, consisted of Charlie's new inner circle taken from various law enforcement agencies.

They were Sweepea, his true love and the representative for the Sheriff's legal department, Danny Ossen, his new number-two man, who was his immediate backup in all things coming into and going out of the Sheriff's Organized Crime Unit, Beth Ruthman, on loan from the FBI, and Blake Goodman, also on loan from the FBI.

The fifth member of the group was Charlie himself, who now asked each of them to make their dinner selections from the menu that had just been presented to them. He told them to splurge and order something expensive as payback for all the danger and hard work that they were getting into. They all sat quietly after he said that and really studied the six-page menu with the deepest concentration.

The Pacific Dining Car was an iconic Central Los Angeles steakhouse with one of the finest reputations, and Charlie thought that this was a good way to kick off the investigation.

The smiling and well-uniformed waitress took their drink orders and sent the instructions to the bar by means of an assistant waiter who was her backup.

Beth Ruthman was the first to order, and she decided to start with a Caesar salad, which the menu said was made of crisp romaine lettuce, parmesan cheese, croutons, and finished with a mild Caesar dressing. For her main course she picked a grilled veal chop, potato gnocchi, mushrooms sautéed with garlic, parsley and veal trimmings.

The waiter complimented her on her selections and went on to Sweetpea, who chose to start with a wedge of iceberg lettuce with imported, aged Roquefort cheese and a creamy dressing with crispy bacon bits, followed by a Colorado rack of lamb sautéed with garlic French beans and rosemary sauce.

Blake Goodman passed on the salad and asked for a porterhouse steak, done medium-well. He ordered a side of French fries and a coke with no ice with his meal.

Danny Ossen ordered what he said was his favorite steak: a filet mignon, well-done, in the usual buttery tender cut that has made this steak an all-time favorite of meat eaters, plus the house salad with Thousand Island dressing.

Charlie was last to order; being the host, he also went for the house salad with ranch dressing on the side and grilled salmon. He also went for French fries to complete his order.

They all made small talk among themselves, which was Charlie's way of getting his new crew well acquainted with each other.

When the meal finally arrived, the conversations immediately ended and some serious eating began.

§

It was about forty minutes later, when all the dishes were cleared away and the desserts had been finished, that Charlie tapped lightly on his water glass to get everyone's attention. It was obvious that Charlie was barely able to control his excitement over the events that were rapidly moving around them all.

Everyone at the table was thinking their own thoughts as they listened to Charlie briefly recap what they had going for them on the undercover investigation.

Once he reviewed all of the events leading up to the moment, answered any questions that came up, until everyone seemed to be on the same page, he started to lay out his plan to get the two FBI agents inside of "the man's" rapidly growing organization.

The bottom line was that Beth and Blake would be in the store location called booth sixty-nine in the Santee Alley shopping area when Federal Agents stormed into the location and arrested everyone present. The attack would not happen until the known person from the organization was working in the back room. His arrest was absolutely the most important part of the plan.

The four of them would be arrested together and booked into the FBI center, and the salesgirl would be quickly released. Her only connection to the criminal organization was that she was unknowingly working as a commissioned salesgirl selling the merchandise laid out in the front of the store's small walk-in area.

§

The heavily armed Federal agents made sure that all the neighboring booths knew that they were there to make the arrests. They stormed the location and took all the electronic equipment and all of the books and papers that they found inside the rear office. Then they formally arrested Beth, Blake and José, who was the person working in the back room and was the main focus and reason for the raid.

The three of them ended up being held in the same holding area, which consisted of two separate cells standing side by side so that conversations between them all could be easily tape-recorded by the listening Sheriff's agents. The planned story line that both Beth and Blake were giving to a very unhappy José was that they came back to his Santee Alley location today to talk to him about making some purchases of special merchandise that they heard that he was selling.

He was completely ignoring their pitch to him until Blake told him that, when he was given his one telephone call that all who were arrested get to make, he called "his people" and told them to use their influence to get them all back on the street immediately. José laughed at them, went over to the two-level bunk beds that were in the corner of the small fifteen-foot-by-fifteen-foot holding cell and went to sleep.

The other two persons sharing his living arrangement settled themselves down quietly with smiles on their faces. Everything was going down just as Charlie Glass had planned. All they were waiting for was their quick release, which should be any minute now, to show the strength and power of who they were. The plan was to impress José, who thought he was going to be charged with something seriously big and that he would be facing prison time.

When the release came within the hour, and they were all released to an attorney known, of course, to Beth and Blake, an absolutely astonished José walked out with them without being charged with anything criminal.

He was most impressed with the power and influence that the two of them obviously had, and they exchanged telephone numbers and agreed to meet in a few days to see if there was some way they could help each other with a bit of business.

CHAPTER THIRTY-ONE

As the old saying goes, Beth and Blake were playing their "new best friend" José from the Santee Alley Mall like a Stradivarius.

They had picked José up at his home in the Westlake area and wined him and dined him with blackened grouper fish and beef oriental with side dishes of rice and a fresh vegetable.

José, who had never been in a fine dining location like the one they were in now, was all smiles and wide eyes as he looked around at the splendid restaurant that the three of them were at. The last time they were all seated together, it had been in two face-to-face jail cells.

Before they left for the restaurant, José had shown off the car that he used to move drugs and money around Los Angeles. He showed them where the special switch was under the dashboard, and how a hidden compartment under the backseat dropped forward, exposing a secret storage area that could easily hold twenty kilos of coke. He then walked them through his home, which was on Twenty-Fifth and Vermont. This was only minutes away from downtown where his outlet store on Santee Street was located.

When Beth asked him straight out if he was working for "the man's" organization, his answer was yes, because "the man's" organization was the only game left in town. Everyone else had been either killed or run off to parts unknown where they could stay away from "the man's" outfit.

José's house had anti-burglar bars covering every door and window in the house. He also showed them an up-to-date computer system that he had bought a few years ago in 1980. He said that he was most impressed with what the new computer could do for him. He carefully closed up his house and got into the back seat of the Rolls Royce sedan that his new friends were using to get them around town.

It was now time for dinner—and then one more surprise stop that Blake told him would be something beyond his wildest dreams. They were going to show him large pieces of luggage filled with one-hundred-dollar bills. This was to show José that they had the money to back up their asking him to help them get into the business. They would offer him a piece of the action in return for his introduction to the right people who could make all of this happen.

José, who had practically finished off a bottle of fine wine all by himself, was rambling on and carrying the conversation along all by himself. He had an attentive audience in Beth and Blake—and in the Sheriff's vehicle that was parked on the nearby street, recording their conversations.

José was saying, with a wide smile on his ugly face, "You must not forget that the people I have agreed to introduce you to have put their trust in me. If there are loses from any of our transactions, I have to eat the loss and cover shortages. The boys will look at me, and I will look at you for the money or your body parts. There is no fooling around with the type of merchandise we are selling and the people we will be dealing with."

He said that the organization likes "to take things in, and not be taken in." He said that he loved to say that expression whenever he could. He also said, in a very serious tone of voice, that mistakes would not be tolerated if they wanted to do business with these people. Everything needed to be talked about by the three of them before they met some of the people that he was planning to introduce them to.

He told them that every agreement would be for cash only, that they would personally have to deliver up front days before they would be receiving the merchandise, which would be guaranteed.

The organization's shipments came to him through Mexico after they had cleared several inspection points on their way from Central America and on into Mexico. The cartel had the okay from Mexico's federal government to ship their product by rail or truck, as it was headed for ultimate buyers in the United Sates.

The cartel would only move its merchandise if they had the Mexican government's protection in the form of many of its police officers, who rode with the convoy up to the United States border where they could see that everything was going smoothly. Without the Mexican police providing protection, the cartel would never think about moving its merchandise.

Beth and Blake dropped off an obviously drunk and sleepy José at his home and went on to report their progress to Charlie Glass.

CHAPTER THIRTY-TWO

Joe Wahl, AKA "the man," had a day off from work and thought it was a good time to review how the operation was going so far with his partner Ernesto. It was agreed that they would meet at Joe's bachelor apartment, located on the beachfront within the city of Santa Monica, a very prosperous community located on the west side of Los Angeles.

Joe could step out of the front lobby of his ocean-front building and walk about one hundred yards and be at the water's edge.

When Joe signed his three-year-lease for his apartment, which faced the ocean front, he had asked to be on the thirteenth floor.

Joe, who was born on the thirteenth of March, always considered this number to be a lucky one for him, and so when he went to sign the three-year-lease for his apartment, he was surprised that there was no thirteenth floor.

The floors on the elevator were all numbered from the lobby to the twelfth floor, and then skipping the number thirteen; the next number was fourteen and so on up to the nineteenth floor which was the penthouse level.

When Joe asked the person who was renting him his apartment about there being no thirteenth floor, he was given a brochure which he found very interesting reading. It read as follows:

Most everyone has had the experience of riding up in

an elevator, listening to the so-called elevator music and seeing that the call buttons for the stops went from the 12th floor directly to the 14th floor. Obviously, the number 13 had become a bad luck number, and Friday the 13th, which was the entire cause of the problem, became a universal bad thing!

The most common rationale was originally a religious one and even though it is an interesting thought, it is not the correct answer to the puzzle about Friday the 13th. Most people believe that the source of this story was when Jesus and His apostles held their last services on a Friday night, which was the thirteenth of the month, when Jesus said that someone present was going to betray him.

It is very easy to see how this event could lead up to an unlucky number thirteen, but even though it seems so right, it was all wrong. Here is the real story as we understand it:

§

A smiling Joe Wahl tucked the interesting papers into his pocket and went about his business.

CHAPTER THIRTY-THREE

Ernesto and Joe Wahl were sitting quietly in Joe's fourteenth-floor apartment looking down on the water as the waves rolled up and down the shoreline. The two men were quite comfortable with each other, as the partnership that they had created was doing wonderful things for them.

It was Joe who opened up the conversation with a wave of his hand and a big smile on his face.

"So, Ernesto, we seem to be off to a good start, do we not? We have effectively eliminated any competitive outsiders from moving in on us, and all we need is a little more time to get our network up and running to where we want it to be. Our accounting reports are telling us that we are making substantial progress in such a short time, and that we are not receiving any lame excuses about late delivery or reduced volume. Unless I am reading the spreadsheet wrong, it seems that we are on the road to making the millions of dollars that we discussed."

A smiling Ernesto was just sitting there quietly nodding his head in agreement with Joe's comments. When he saw that his partner was waiting for him to jump in to the conversation, he carefully opened up his end of the discussion by looking at his notes on the spreadsheet laid out before him on the coffee table.

Ernesto started off by saying that according to the latest numbers, they had pulled in just shy of a one-million-dollar profit for the past six weeks. "These numbers are good considering that we are just developing our outlets and street locations after cleaning up the competition. Do you remember my cousin José Creto, who runs our outlet store over at the Downtown Santee Street Mall? José's complaint is the same one that I am getting from almost all of our outlets, and that is that he could triple his sales and his bottom-line profits if he only had more merchandise to sell. All our guys are doing is complaining that they have the orders, but they have no way to fill them. The demand is there, but our supplies are not."

The two of them spent the rest of the evening going over the numbers from the various locations, and they concluded that if they had more merchandise to sell, they could triple their profits almost overnight.

At the end of their brief meeting, as Ernesto was getting ready to ring for the elevator that would take him from Joe's penthouse to the lobby, he mentioned his cousin José Creto once again.

José had told Ernesto that he was approached by a very high-end, very classy couple who had walked into his location at the Santee downtown outlet. José had investigated them and their claims that they could deliver huge quantities of merchandise at a reasonable price, but he hesitated to go beyond the talking stage before he talked with Ernesto for the authority to go forward with the discussion.

They had made a most interesting offer for José to pass on to his bosses. They offered a steady supply of Colombian product for the introductory price of a hundred thousand dollars for a delivery of six hundred and seventy-five individual package units. José said that he penciled in the cost of the product and the profit that they would make if they sold it at their outlets on the street, and came up with the interesting number of three million dollars in profit per delivery.

The couple, whom he called Beth and Blake, said that they

could deliver this quantity upon a weekly basis, and if this was of interest to José's people, the offer would be open for discussion for a time limit of thirty days.

Cousin José had brought a sample of the merchandise with him, and Ernesto had it tested at one of their local labs. It checked out to be top-grade, never cut.

Cousin José said that Beth and Blake would take care of him in return for his introduction, so in that way there would be no cost to Ernesto if he was interested in meeting with them and possibly setting up a chain of supply from Colombia to Los Angeles.

An interested Joe Wahl invited Ernesto to come back into his apartment so that they could discuss this promising development further. There was definitely potential here; maybe this could fill in the shortages that they were experiencing.

CHAPTER THIRTY-FOUR

Charlie Glass was still a very happy man. He was running on the excitement that he had previously created when he brought in Beth Ruthman and Blake Goodman from the FBI to work with himself, Danny Ossen, and the entire narcotics division of the Los Angeles Sheriff's Department.

He had just returned from meeting with one of the top assistants to William Webster, director of the Federal Bureau of Investigation in Washington. He was given the go-ahead to make use of whatever money was needed to destroy the rapidly growing drug empire that was gaining great traction in Southern California.

It was a most professional meeting, and at no time was Charlie asked to provide names of anyone he was working with, either undercover or within his own department. The concern was that somehow or other a name could be leaked out, and that would be a complete disaster for everyone involved.

The money that was needed to make all of their plans work would be specially marked one-hundred-dollar bills that could be easily traced back to the source as the cash was used to pay for illegal drugs coming into the United States. Having these unlimited funds was the key to Charlie's whole planned operation. With the blessing of the FBI behind him, he was now prepared to move things forward.

And possibly one of the most interesting things to come out

of all of this was the fact that Joe Wahl, they now knew beyond a shadow of a doubt, was the number-one person leading the new organized-crime family. Joe seemed to be a most capable guy, as he did whatever he had to do for his drug group, while he continued to work at his job at the Los Angeles Sheriff's Department and do it well.

In order to make a strong case that would stick against Joe Wahl, Ernesto and their other known and not-known associates, they needed to create a tracking system so that they could follow the marked cash as it was moved about. Tracking money through the accounts of others was a bitch to follow, in that the money would be deposited locally and then transferred to other countries and then dispersed all over the world.

According to what they were now seeing, the local money was being circulated in an extremely clever way and laundered in such a manner that tracking it was most difficult and almost impossible. Joe Wahl, operating as "the man," owned outright several downtown Los Angeles hotels. His accountants would prepare records to show that every room was occupied almost every night, even though the hotels were virtually empty most of the time. This allowed them to push their illegal dope money through the books as hotel revenue. And with all the hotel's legitimate write-offs, no taxes had to be paid and the profits from dope money became legitimized. Someone very clever had come up with this almost perfect scheme of money laundering. It was most impressive.

§

Ernesto called for a dinner meeting at his home, which was located in the heart of Beverly Hills.

He had only recently moved into the exclusive Beverly Hills neighborhood because he realized that it would be a wonderful place to invest in real estate with much of his ill-gotten gains. He was fascinated by the history of the city and he hired a publicity firm to detail out all the necessary past doings within the city, so that he could be comfortable investing inside the city limits.

Within his expensive new home, which was located at the corner of Wilshire Boulevard and La Cienega, were several framed and beautifully put-together stories and pictures about the history of the City of Beverly Hills that he wanted to make his new home.

§

Beverly Hills is a city in Los Angeles County, California, United States of America. It is surrounded by the cities of Los Angeles and West Hollywood.

It was originally a Spanish ranch where lima beans were grown. It was incorporated in 1914 by a group of investors who had failed to find the oil that they were looking for. Instead they found water and eventually decided to develop it into a town.

By the early 1980s, its population had grown to over 30,000 people.

It is or has been home to many actors and celebrities, and its area includes many world-famous locations such as the Rodeo Drive shopping district and the Beverly Hills oilfields.

§

EARLY HISTORY

Gaspar de Portola arrived in the area that would later become Beverly Hills on August 3, 1769. To get there, he had to travel over native trails which followed the present-day Wilshire Boulevard.

By the 1880s, the ranch had been subdivided into parcels of 75 acres and was bought up by "Anglos" (white folks) from Los Angeles and the east coast. Henry Hammel and Andrew H. Denker acquired most of it and used it for farming lima beans.

In 1906 the first house was built in one of many all-white planned communities. Restrictive covenants prohibited non-whites from owning or renting property unless they were employed as servants by white residents. It was also forbidden to sell or rent property to Jews in Beverly Hills.

In 1919 Douglas Fairbanks and Mary Pickford bought land and built a mansion in 1921 and named it Pickfair. The glamour associated with Fairbanks and Pickford, as well as other movie stars who built mansions nearby, contributed to the growing appeal of Beverly Hills.

In the 1950s and 1960s, the city became the home of Elvis Presley, Frank Sinatra, Dean Martin, Tony Curtis, Tony Martin, and Ray Charles. More recent residents were President Richard Nixon, Jennifer Aniston, David Spade and Vera Wang.

CHAPTER THIRTY-FIVE

Ernesto served an exquisite lunch for his three guests, who were his cousin José Creto, who ran one of the better distributing locations, and Beth Ruthman and Blake Goodman, who were potential suppliers of the highly desired Central American drugs that were in short supply in all of Southern California.

And most important was the special guest star: a simple traveling suitcase filled with hundreds of small, carefully wrapped packages of the narcotic product that they had brought to show to Ernesto. It was obvious that Beth and Blake were here to impress Ernesto with the quality and quantity of the drugs for import.

The lunch was pleasant, and everyone appeared anxious to make the deal that would make them all into wealthy players in the biggest game in town. The only disturbing point that came up during the wonderful dessert of pie and different flavors of ice cream, was that Beth and Blake were unwilling to close the deal with Ernesto.

"Ernesto," Blake was saying, "you are pleasant, good-humored, smart and quite knowledge-able, but you are still not the number-one player in this drama, who we need to personally meet and make the deal with. Your cousin José Creto knows how to get in touch with us, and he also has seen first-hand how we are able to control the law enforcement agencies that will be looking at all of us. And now we bid you a good day."

With a friendly smile on their faces, the two North American drug dealers left the room, walked over to their parked car and drove away.

Joe Wahl, who was sitting and listening from the room adjacent to the dining room where they had lunch, waited for Ernesto to also send José Creto on his way, so that he could walk into the kitchen unobserved and partake of the excellent leftovers from the luncheon that had just been served.

José Creto had to leave the home before Joe Wahl would present himself. Inside the entire organization, only Ernesto had the authority needed for seeing Joe Wahl face to face. To everyone else he was just a voice, and no one knew who he was, and that was the way Joe wanted to keep things.

Between bites of the excellent food that was still on display on the table, Joe was saying to Ernesto that he wanted him to get some answers to the questions still surrounding these two people. "Who are they really? Where did they come from and why? Who do we know and trust that can speak up for them?"

"They came from nowhere and have not given us any real proof of who they are and what they can really do for us. In the meantime, go ahead and distribute the contents of the suitcase and get back some comments on the results. Let us create a desire for the really good stuff that we all think is in that suitcase, in case we do make a deal with them. I shall personally meet with them, in your presence, if everything you check into comes out positively. We could be on the edge of the biggest deal in our lifetime, or it could be a big bust."

CHAPTER THIRTY-SIX

Again, not trusting that any of their conversations within the Sheriff's station was secure, Danny and Charlie shared their thoughts over at one of the nearby Chinese restaurants that was within easy walking distance from their offices. It was Danny Ossen who came up with the plan that would make it all come together.

Charlie sat back and listened as Danny reviewed the progress that they had made up to that moment. He said that he believed that "the man," as Joe Wahl was now being referred to, would put out his feelers to see if Beth and Blake were for real.

Danny had spent all of his time yesterday going through the records from the LAPD and his own Sheriff's Department that dealt with the dozens of minor drug dealers who were caught red-handed pushing illegal substances on the streets of Los Angeles. Danny was telling Charlie that they needed insiders from "the man's" organization to help establish the credentials for Beth and Blake as reliable suppliers of the "product." Without verification of their working credentials from their own people, Ernesto would never recommend doing business with these new people who had come knocking at their door.

It was Danny's idea to make a deal with the dozen or more locked-up drug dealers who were sitting in the Sheriff's and the LAPD's holding cells, just waiting on their trial dates that would send them off to jail. He thought that they should release a few of them at a time and let them go back to the streets, only this time wearing a wire twenty-four hours a day, so that they could be monitored at all times.

The deal would be that their criminal records showing their recent arrests would be wiped, and they would be free to leave the city, which they would have to do within a thirty-day period from carrying out their part of the release bargain. They would be supplied with large amounts of money that they would say were their profits from dealing with Beth and Blake's inexpensive narcotics. Of course, they would have to give the organization their share of the profits from the sale, but the money was plentiful and everyone, at least by outward appearances, would seem happy. Danny further proposed that they keep up the appearances of drug dealing for at least forty-five days in order to give them time to build up their reputation and make easy money for one and all.

While Danny was speaking, Charlie had been carefully listening, and at the same time had been eating his luncheon of Chinese food. When Danny was finished, it was Charlie's turn to talk while Danny dug into his lunch.

Charlie told him that he was very pleased with Danny's plan, and he would authorize everything accordingly. He only added that the money Beth and Blake would be handing out would be carefully marked bills, so that they could be entered into evidence when they finally got to court.

He again stressed that Beth and Blake would only do business with "the man," and until a meeting with him took place, the undercover agents would have to stay in town. He anticipated a six-month-minimum time frame until the program became smooth enough to almost run itself.

In the best of moods, the two detectives finished up their lunches, read their fortune cookies, and walked back to the station to get things rolling.

CHAPTER THIRTY-SEVEN

A very busy ninety days had passed, and we find Lead Detective Charlie Glass entering the home of the recognized leader of the South American/Mexican importers of fine products, which everyone knew included narcotics among the many products that it brought in from California's southernmost neighbor.

Charlie was there at the invitation of the president of the importers' council to discuss the upstart organization called "the man" group. It was obviously bad for their business having their field agents either killed or absorbed into this new and highly aggressive narcotic-selling organization.

Over the years, the LAPD and the Sheriff's Department had made their peace with this group of importers, who kept a very low profile while they sold their illegal products. Little if any violence had occurred over the years, and only recently had their industry become of interest to the FBI and the local police agencies because of their selling the same products as "the man" group. The problem was that "the man" group used extreme violence, which caught the eye of everyone, instead of the old way of doing business, which let money do the talking.

Charlie was there to discuss getting some possible help from them as he tried to get rid of Joe Wahl and his very aggressive tactics.

Charlie followed the exquisitely dressed butler through the

wealth and splendor of the huge house's hardwood floors and carved wooden statues, fountains and a suit or two of armor. He noted among the many original paintings as he walked along the long hallway, an original Van Gogh that had a small spotlight shining down upon it.

After a long hike, the butler delivered him into a wing of the house that had apparently been converted into corporate office space. There were half a dozen efficient-looking people working in the cubicles. Telephones with digital ringtones chirruped in the background, as a sound system played soft-rock music. As he went past a break room, he got the smell of fresh coffee, and finally the butler stopped at the end of the long hallway and held open one of the doors for Charlie to enter.

Charlie found himself inside an inner office that was complete with a secretary's desk being used by a stunning young woman whose blond hair was held back in a ponytail and who wore a conservative gray pantsuit. As he entered, she rose with a polite, impersonal smile that could have taken first prize in any number of competitive beauty pageants. "Sir, if you'll come this way, please, Diane is ready to see you now."

She went over to the door on the wall behind her desk, knocked once, and opened it enough to say, "Detective Charlie Glass is here to see you."

A very soft feminine voice answered in the affirmative, and the escort opened the door all the way. Charlie entered and the door closed quietly behind him.

Diane Jones's office had a few things in common with the front offices that Charlie had walked through. It had the same rich furnishings, though its style was generally darker. The resemblance ended there. This office was a working office. It had mail stacked neatly on a corner of her big desk and the work-table against one wall was fully engulfed with a paperwork anarchy that threatened to take over the entire room, but order had been strongly imposed, guided by an obviously, iron will.

Diane Jones sat quietly behind her huge desk and looked at him.

She was wearing a silk business suit of the purest white, cut close to the flawless lines of her body. The cut of the suit elegantly displayed her figure and contrasted sharply with long blue-black hair, which hung in waves past her shoulders. Her features had the classically immortal beauty of a Greek statue, balancing sheer beauty with feminine strength, intelligence and perception. Her eyes were a deep, warm gray, framed by thick, sooty lashes, and just looking at her full soft mouth made Charlie's lips twitch and tingle as they begged for an introduction to them.

The meeting lasted for a little over an hour, with Charlie doing most of the talking, and Diane jotting down points of interest from what he was saying upon a little yellow pad.

Charlie acknowledged the fact that the LAPD and his own Sheriff's Department were well aware that among the many legal business deals that Diane's company was involved in, there were a few illegal activities thrown into the mix that dealt with narcotics being sold on the streets of Southern California. Both Diane and Charlie were veterans of the street-gang wars, and each had learned to live with them and each other in a civilized manner.

The small amounts of the imported drugs that Diane's company supplied to the streets were accepted as a necessary evil which did as much good as bad. The bad was that they sold the narcotics, and the good was that violence in the form of war between the street gangs were kept to an acceptable minimum, and this was an ongoing good thing for many years, with the law enforcement agencies and Diane's people being careful not to step on each other's toes. This keep the lid on violence in the city, and everyone lived with it.

All of the above was true until the organization that had recently invaded the city under the guidance of "the man" began to murder the competition and one by one take over their customers by giving them a choice of doing business with this newest player or simply dying. Diane and the companies that she controlled, realizing that their huge money-making machine was being threatened by this newcomer to the business, sent out a private signal to Charlie to come to her office, where they hopefully could mutually help each other with the new problem that was now running wild in the streets.

Their meeting was pleasant and precise. Diane and her organization would make sure that the word got out onto the streets how reliable, steady and well-funded Beth and Blake were. She agreed to help establish the credibility of the two undercover agents with the understanding that once they had cleaned out this nest of evil vipers, all would return to business as usual, which meant that the Sheriff's Department and the LAPD would once again turn a blind eye to Diane's street operations.

Both seemed satisfied with their new verbal agreement.

Charlie was quite sure that their meeting had to have been recorded by Diane' people but he was comfortable with that because he was personally wired up and connected to the Sheriff's Department, which was making a recording of everything done within the confines of their buildings.

Diane promised to get the word out as soon as it could possibly be done, and get the two agents accepted into the underground crowd.

They shook hands upon a done deal, and then Charlie allowed himself to be led out of the offices and back out into the huge parking lot that surrounded the building complex, with watchtowers and guards who watched the perimeter twenty-four hours a day, seven days a week.

CHAPTER THIRTY-EIGHT

Suddenly, about ten days later, everything that they had been talking about started to move on the case that was being called "the man."

The Los Angeles Police Department called it that, and Diane from the Mexican State Importers called it that, but when written or spoken about at any Sheriff's locations, this very special case was being referred to as Operation Narco, and it was a one-hundred-percent sealed-off case with the only access to it given to Detective Charlie Glass and Detective Danny Ossen. It had to be handled this way due to the fact that Detective Joe Wahl had complete and full entry into all cases not marked in this manner.

Detective Wahl was seen always going into and out of the various case files that were open to one and all. No one other than Charlie and Danny thought that there was anything unusual about it. Charlie and Danny thought that he was probably looking for any new references to his organization.

That special understanding that Charlie and Diane had come to in their private meeting was beginning to work out well. It was definitely worth the time and effort being put in by the two of them to see that things moved along as planned. Her street dealers and the Los Angeles Police Department's and the Sheriff's Department's released minor felons all seemed to reach the streets within a few days of each other, and things were flowing along quite well. Diane's guys were especially motivated by legally being able to help get rid of their street competition, and the released felons saw a great way out of not having to do jail time while making themselves some easy street-money doing what they were always doing anyway.

Both groups loved picking up some cash for themselves as they flashed their increased cash flow around town as part of the deal to sing the praises of Beth and Blake's organization. Both law enforcement agencies' and Diane's guys were given five thousand dollars each in marked one-hundred-dollar bills, and instructed to circulate them around as they talked up the new suppliers whose reputation was growing stronger day by day.

Whatever was being circulated on the streets was confirmed by the wires that everyone was forced to wear. If anyone took them off or tampered with them in any way, they were subject either to arrest again or being fired if they were Diane's guys. It was a win-win situation for everyone if all the players followed their instructions.

And finally, Ernesto contacted Beth and Blake about having the meeting that they wanted with himself and his partner known as "the man." The time and the location would be given to them on the same day as the meeting, but it would be on an extremely short notice so as not to allow anything to get fouled up. Beth and Blake agreed to the setup, and went about doing whatever it was that they were doing to keep busy.

By means of a private telephone line used exclusively by Charlie Glass, Beth called to catch him up on the latest developments in the case. Final plans were made and the telephone connection ended with everyone knowing what they were going to be doing to help wrap up this most important of cases.

Charlie made sure that the FBI and other parties "of interest" were kept in the loop.

CHAPTER THIRTY-NINE

The meeting was called for two in the afternoon at one of the downtown Los Angeles hotels owned and operated by Ernesto on behalf of himself and Joe Wahl.

The two men were seated in the business office located on the third floor of the nine-story building. The room was spotlessly clean and in perfect order, since that was pretty much the description for Ernesto himself, who worked out of this office as his main headquarters.

Ernesto had just finished making his presentation to Joe Wahl, which laid out for the two of them the who, what, where and when that any of their own people had had personal contact or had spoken to people within the organization who had done some business with Blake Goodman and Beth Ruthman.

There were no negatives in anything that Ernesto pulled up from his paperwork and presented to Joe Wahl. Ernesto was perfectly satisfied that the two sellers under discussion were for real, and truly wanted to break into the strong market that Los Angeles offered them.

Joe Wahl, on the other hand, was not as pleased as Ernesto was. He kept telling Ernesto that the paperwork that they had in front of them was too clean and too perfect. There was no evidence of any of their employees ripping them off. No evidence of the usual cash disappearing as it always did. No evidence that everything was anything less than perfect. And being this close to perfect bothered Joe.

Over Ernesto's objections, Joe Wahl walked out on their meeting. All he would say was that something did not feel right to him. He said that he smelled a rat, which meant that something was too good with the offer that was being made to them. He wanted more time before he committed. Joe said to Ernesto, as he left the room, that Ernesto should make the deal on his own if they would do so without himself being there, or if his not being there broke down the deal, then he was supposed to tell them to continue with the street sales just as they had been doing, and they would get together another day.

Joe Wahl said that he needed a bit more time to see how things were going with the regular day-to-day operations. He did not feel comfortable yet with getting such a good price and having Beth and Blake actually provide street salespeople to move the merchandise for them. When a deal is too good, it usually isn't.

An unhappy Ernesto went down to the lobby to meet and greet his two guests, who would be having lunch with him.

When the breakdown of the meeting was reported to him, an extremely disappointed Charlie Glass called for an emergency meeting within the next day or two to discuss the latest happenings on this case that seemed to be going nowhere. Joe Wahl was too street-wise and too intelligent to jump into something that seemed too good of a deal to be for real. He did not get to be where he was by not trusting his instincts.

Charlie was thinking that he and Danny Ossen might be a bit too close to everything that was going on, and perhaps they needed fresh viewpoints. As such, he had asked a lot of people to attend a most secret meeting that would be held in the FBI building located in Westwood, California, about thirty minutes from downtown Los Angeles. The security would be extremely tight, and he could get some insights from his long-time friend and associate Fred Bloom, who had worked himself up to a position of third assistant to the Los Angeles Branch director.

He had given the job of getting everyone on his list that he felt he needed to attend this emergency meeting to Sweetpea, who would also be there to take the notes of the meeting as well as organizing the meeting room. He would have her ask the following "heavy hitters" to be there: Fred Bloom from the FBI, Danny Ossen, his number two, Beth Ruthman, Blake Goodman and himself.

CHAPTER FORTY

The meeting was held in the large assembly hall of the FBI building as planned.

It was Blake Goodman who took a few minutes and explained in detail about the meeting that ended up with just Ernesto, instead of Ernesto and "the man," who they all knew was Joe Wahl. Everything that preceded the meeting had been done perfectly and by the book, but everything had fallen apart when something spooked Joe Wahl, who had walked out on the meeting before it really began.

Danny Ossen, speaking for his group of the Sheriff's people who were present, wanted Fred Bloom, their FBI host, to offer some thoughts on where they were going wrong as they tried to put together a case against Joe Wahl.

Everyone turned and looked up at the now-standing Fred Bloom, who smiled at everyone in the pleasant and easy manner that was his claim to fame within his department. Fred, in his soft and moderated tone of voice, nailed the problem right on the head. At least that is what everyone said when they got together after the meeting.

Fred said that they had to up the cost of the product. "Don't ever be the low man! If they need your product as much as you say they do, they will appreciate it more if they have to pay more for it. You want to take away anything that looks too easy to Joe

Wahl. Joe came up the hard way, as we all did, and anything too good or too easy gives him an immediate red flag warning. Set up some hurdles that he will have to make a personal effort himself to meet. In other words, dirty up the deal and get down to his level." With a big smile on his face, Fred Bloom waved a little hand wave and exited the room.

It took over an hour before the rest of the group agreed upon a new strategy that seemed to fit the advice given to them by the FBI's chief planner for domestic affairs. They all agreed that they were now going to play hard-to-get with the narcotics that they were offering up for sale.

They started talking about how to bait and switch their product, or as Sweetpea later wrote in her notebook: "offer up the product after taking their money and take our own sweet time about delivering what we promised. This will make them sweat a bit."

CHAPTER FORTY-ONE

Several months went by and nothing of any importance on the case was happening. There was absolutely nothing heard from Ernesto or anyone else in his organization.

The number of narcotics floating around in Southern California was dwindling rapidly, and the only sources that were able to meet supply and demand were the Beth/Bruce people who allowed only a small amount of their FBI-borrowed narcotics to go out into the field. It was just enough to show that they had sources but not enough to ease the pressure that was being felt on the streets. The thought was to dry up the normal flow into and out of the city until shortages would push Joe Wahl's group to be getting desperate for supplies. It was a situation where Joe Wahl had the customers but no product, and would have to secure a source somewhere soon, or his customers would be going out of the city to meet their ever-growing needs.

And so, with this new strategy in place, it was not at all surprising that Beth and Blake received a telephone call from Ernesto, who left a message that he needed a return call as soon as possible. He said that an urgent matter had just come up, and that he needed to discuss it with them. Would they kindly set up a meeting in the next few days, and he would come to them at whatever location and time would work for them.

This sounded wonderful to Charlie, when he heard about the

telephone call from Ernesto. He was much impressed with his contact at the FBI who had helped them formulate the strategy that they would now be working under. It seemed that his friend had pretty much predicted what was now seemingly about to happen. It was great having someone who could guide them in this new game of cat-and-mouse that they were entering into. Charlie always thought that it was good to have all sorts of friends and contacts in all the right places. This one was one of the good things coming back to him for all the lunches and banquets that he had been attending for these many years.

Charlie had Beth and Blake continue being highly visible as they worked the central downtown area of Los Angeles. He wanted the word to get out that even though they had doubled the price of their narcotics, their supply was still very plentiful. Anyone who wanted to be considered a player in the great game of narcotics in the City of Los Angeles had to come to their seemingly unlimited supply of product that they had quietly acquired from their secret partner in the operation, the Federal Bureau of Investigation.

Charlie's immediate problem was where to hold the all-important meeting that Ernesto was calling for. It had to be in a location that they could completely control and where they could set up a series of recording devices that were definitely needed for the case if they ever hoped to nail Joe Wahl and Ernesto.

Again, it was Sweetpea who came up with the answer. Sweetpea suggest that the meeting should take place at the restaurant overlooking the small harbor at Marina del Rey where she had recently had a very pleasant dining experience. She had been there at a luncheon for a friend who was about to retire from the Los Angeles County Department of Beaches and Harbors.

It was when she was driving over to the restaurant that she had noted that there was a Sheriff's station nearby. With the Sheriff's Department working hand in hand with them on the Joe Wahl case, it would be easy enough to get the Sheriff's permission to install their recording equipment at this location that they supervised. Danny Ossen made the necessary call to the Sheriff's office and received the authorization to set up whatever they wanted in connection with this case.

Charlie personally put a call into Blake Goodman and told him to set up the meeting in one week and have it at the address that he was going to give to him. This one-week delay would allow them to set up the equipment that they would use to record the lunch conversation.

Blake said that he would make the date right away and get back to Charlie with Ernesto's confirmation.

Charlie told Blake to ask if "the man," who had walked out on their last meeting, would be coming to this one. They both thought that this would not happen, but it never hurts to ask.

§

It was one week later when the three of them were shown to the best table in the dining room. Beth, Blake and Ernesto were all seated right next to the huge glass window that looked directly down upon the beautiful sail- and motorboats moving about in the blue waters of the marina. The view was amazingly beautiful. The golden sunlight of the early afternoon reflected in the rippling waters as many of the boats passed directly under their window. After the several meetings that they had had, the three of them seemed to be the very best of friends as they ordered from the menu and watched the boats move about in the blue waters of the beautiful marina.

It was Ernesto who opened up the conversation that they were all interested in. He told them that if they could come to an agreement now about quantity and prices, then he would have the senior partner present at the next meeting. He apologized for his missing partner at their last luncheon engagement and said that he was not comfortable at that time as to who they were. A great deal of investigation had gone on quietly, and as a result he was here today to finalize the agreement that he hoped would be profitable for all of them for many years to come.

Blake was playing the role of the easy-to-get-along-with guy. Beth was playing at being the hard-nosed bitch, and playing it perfectly. "How do we know that we are not wasting our time again today? The last time we met, it was very embarrassing to be walked out on. If the arrangement that we are going to come to today does not have the boss available to close it, then this will be the last time, and I will personally see to it that the word gets around that you are not reliable and do not keep your word."

After Blake calmed her down, and Ernesto just sat there watching the attractive young lady work herself up into a minor rage, then they all relaxed again between mouthfuls of the excellent luncheon that was served to them.

Ernesto wanted to pay the original prices that were quoted to him at the last meeting, where his partner had walked out and left the details to him.

Blake said that the cost of doing business had gone up tremendously and that the best that they could do was to give him a twenty-five percent discount off the price that they were giving to everyone else in today's market.

Thinking out loud so that they could follow his thoughts, Ernesto agreed to the price. Even with the increase in the cost, the twenty-five percent discount would allow him to undercut the other sellers of the product.

Even Beth was impressed when Ernesto told them of the volume that he wanted to buy. She told him that the numbers that he wanted just for his operation, were about the equal of all the other dealers that they were doing business with.

It was Blake who told him that they would need ten percent down, in cash, at the next meeting. And, he said, at this next meeting they were planning on meeting "the man" up close and personal. If he was a no-show, or even worse, if they backed out of the deal, they would spread the word out on the street that they were not reliable to do business with, and they would stop at nothing to ruin their reputation and put them out of business.

A smiling Ernesto accepted all their angry words, and with smiles and toasts with the soft drinks that they were all drinking, assured them that everything would be perfect. He went on to say that they should not be angry with himself or his partner, because deals like this take a lot of time and investigation before everything gets cleared up.

They finished up their lunch telling stories and adventures that they all had in their life in the business that they had all chosen for themselves. As they were all waiting for their cars to be brought up by the valet, Ernesto promised that their final meeting would be scheduled within the next ten days or so, and that he would be in contact with them as to where and when. It would be held with just the four of them, and they would finalize whatever details needed to be worked out.

With hugs and handshakes the two cars drove off into the beautiful afternoon sunshine that enclosed the Los Angeles Marina.

CHAPTER FORTY-TWO

Everything was looking really good on the case that they were building against Ernesto and Joe Wahl. The only thing missing was the final meeting where Joe Wahl himself was going to appear. Without Joe being there, the whole case would be going nowhere and that was Charlie's biggest concern. Would Joe show us for this last meeting or was there something that might have scared him off? What worried Charlie, was that Joe might "smell a rat" in the upcoming deal and once again not personally come to the big meeting.

Special agents Beth and Blake had definitely established the appearance that they were the only really high-quality sellers of the wanted merchandise, and the chances were good that both Ernesto and Joe would appear in order to protect their business. But without Joe Wahl present at the meeting, there would be no deal, and then the organization that Ernesto and Joe had put together would still be ongoing.

Knowing that this was the only shot that he had to put down the entire organization, Charlie went ahead and called in all of the necessary manpower to ensure that this operation was going to be successful. The FBI, the LAPD and his own Sheriff's Department all had their hand in the operation, but it was Charlie who was leading everyone and calling all the shots. Charlie had personally talked with everyone involved and had received commitments from each of them that they would come running when he called. Everyone wanted to get this problem behind them.

While they all were waiting, life proceeded in the usual manner.

§

It was on the ninth day that Beth and Blake received a telephone call from Ernesto. The meeting was to be held next Monday morning at ten o'clock. The meeting place was to be on the unfinished roof area for the U.S. Bank Tower Building, located on Fifth Street in central L.A.

Ernesto told them that they were to come alone, and that the meeting would be between the four of them only. He told them that he and his boss would be bringing one hundred thousand dollars in large bills to start up the initial ordering of the product. He said that Blake did not have to bring any more samples to the meeting. What they had originally given to them was tested as high quality, and they were completely satisfied.

He also asked them to put together a schedule for the first delivery, and when and how often they would be bringing in more product. They wanted to work up some sort of distribution schedule and needed the time frame in-put.

Naturally, the telephones that Blake and Beth were using were tied into several recording devices at the FBI. Nothing was to be directly done on the case by the Sheriff or LAPD since Joe might have someone connected to him that would be listening to all calls.

The conversation that was now recorded by the FBI was sufficient evidence to make an arrest of Ernesto, but nothing was known about the fourth party to the meeting. Was he going to show up, or skip out like he did the last time? Everyone would be thinking about this, and the time slowly passed.

Sweetpea did the research upon their meeting place, and it became obvious why this particular location was chosen. The building was in its final days of construction, and the remaining work still to be done was on the ground floor. There should be no workers or anyone else on the roof area at the time of the meeting.

The building, which would top out at one thousand and eighteen feet, was located at 633 West Fifth Street in Los Angeles. The official name for the building was the Library Towers First Interstate Bank World Center, and the roof where the meeting with Ernesto and his friend was going to be held was seventy-three stories high. That would make this the tallest building in Los Angeles.

CHAPTER FORTY-THREE

Since the meeting that was going to take place on the roof of the Interstate Bank Building was not scheduled until next Monday, Charlie had plenty of time to get things set up, with well-hidden spy cameras everywhere. The cameras needed to be set up to cover every single foot of the huge roof area in overlapping patterns, because there was no way to know exactly where the four-person meeting would take place.

Charlie and his number-two guy, Danny Ossen, would be somewhere down the street, where they would be close but out of the way, as well as Roberto Sanchez, whom Charlie had thought might have been Ernesto's partner. The LAPD and the FBI also had representatives that would positively be there.

They were all going to meet about two blocks away in a local coffee shop, where they would patiently wait until they got a call from one of the plainclothes detectives who were wandering around near the entrance to the building and watching for the four players in the drama to show up.

There was a special control room set up in the basement that would absorb all the videos and conversations that would be going on roof side.

Late Friday afternoon, Charlie was delivered a note from one of the installers of the special recording equipment. It was signed by the team leader of the crew, and it only had one word on a single sheet of paper. It read "COMPLETED."

Charlie folded up the note and put it in his pocket. On his way out for the weekend he said good-by to the few detectives who were at their writing desks working on their paperwork. He returned Joe's hand-wave as he rang for the elevator that would take him to the basement where his car was parked. He had a free Saturday and Sunday that he planned to spend with Sweetpea. Monday morning could not come soon enough for him.

§

Monday morning had finally arrived, and by eight-thirty everyone who had been invited was present. Coffee, donuts and very little conversation was going on within the group sitting quietly when Danny Ossen's two-way radio went off.

It was from one of the plainclothes detectives, who was watching the only entrance into the plaza. He reported that the last couple to enter the lobby was Ernesto and another man that he knew to be Joe Wahl. He reported that they were standing by the elevators waiting for one to arrive.

When the elevator arrived, the two men stepped in and the door closed behind them. As soon as the elevator door closed, the plainclothes detective stood and watched the elevator's numbering system until it finally stopped at the floor that the indicator showed as the roof. There was a few moments' pause, and then the elevator started to head down to the main lobby.

While it was heading down, the detective left the lobby and went outside, where he stood on the other side of the clear glass doors that gave him a good view of the elevators. He wanted to be sure that the elevator was empty, which it was, meaning that the two men had stepped off on the roof area. That was when he made the call, which ended up with Charlie and all his companions walking toward the Tower Building.

When they arrived there was a dispatcher from the basement recording team waiting for them. He told Charlie that his supervisor, who was overseeing the recordings being made of the conversation going on at the rooftop, said that the two undercover agents were doing a wonderful job building up the case. The recording had Joe Wahl and Ernesto talking specifically about how they would soon be distributing what they were calling "the product." The recording supervisor, who was an expert on gathering self-incriminating evidence, said to tell Charlie that they had more than enough evidence, and that it was now time for an arrest to be made.

Without thanking the messenger, all of the men dashed out of the waiting room and headed for the bank of elevators that were all being held open by twenty armed FBI, Sheriff's deputies, and LAPD officers.

As soon as Charlie and crew were inside the elevators, the buttons were pushed and several moments that seemed like forever went by as they were being whisked upward to the open roof area. Finally, the doors opened with several loud dings, and in moments the officers, with their weapons drawn, spread out across the roof top and then walked in a fairly straight line as they crossed the roof to where the three males and one female were standing and looking directly at them.

They were standing at the far end of the roof, and one of them took an extra few steps and sat down on the ledge of the rooftop. He was sitting with his legs swinging over the side and his body was turned sideways so that he could speak to the intruders.

Without a word being spoken, Beth and Blake stepped away from where they were, and passed through the line of the advancing officers. Only Ernesto stood perfectly still, as if he could not understand what was happening around him. Two officers forcefully led him away from the area, where they searched him and then handcuffed him to a steel construction beam.

Everyone, the deputies, the undercover agents, the FBI and the Sheriff's men, all stood perfectly still with their pistols held pointing down and at their sides.

It was Charlie Glass who stepped forward alone to where Joe Wahl was sitting quietly waiting for him. Charlie stopped about five feet away from Joe in case it was his plan to use Charlie as a hostage. It obviously was not Joe's plan, as he just sat there quietly, smoking a cigarette.

There was not much to say, and Charlie simply asked in a voice that was hard and extremely unpleasant in its tone, "Why, Joe?"

With a half-smile on his face, Joe turned around a little bit more toward Charlie as he calmly said, "Because I could."

With those words on his lips, Joe Wahl pushed himself off of the ledge of the roof and started his fall of one thousand and eighteen feet.